Rendered Invisible

*Stories Of Blacks and Whites,
Love and Death*

Frank E. Dobson, Jr.

Plain View Press
P. O. 42255
Austin, TX 78704

plainviewpress.net
sb@plainviewpress.net
512-441-2452

Copyright Frank E. Dobson, Jr. , 2010. All rights reserved.
ISBN: 978-1-935514-35-0
Library of Congress Number: 2010923420

Cover art by Stephen Babalola
Cover design by Susan Bright

Acknowledgements

Gratitude to the following publications for publishing these stories: "Homeless M.F." in *Warpland: A Journal of Black Literature and Ideas*. Vol. No. 1, 1995, 21-24; "Junior Ain't" in *Proverbs for the People: An Anthology of African American Fiction*, Kensignton Press, 2003, 84-86; and "Black Messiahs Die" in *The Vanderbilt Review*, Vol. XX, Spring 2005, 134-42.

To my wife, Dioncia

Contents

The fact is that you carry a part of your sickness within you, at least I do as an invisible man.

Ralph Ellison, *Invisible Man*

Rendered Invisible

Chapter One

Barbershop talk—

In the fall of 1980, a pathological white racist murdered black males in and around Buffalo, NY, my hometown. The men he killed ranged in age from 14 to 71. The case, called the .22-Caliber Killer, received relatively little national attention then or since. This is the witness of my friend, Johnny, who lived through the killing spree. After all these years, he told us his story. We just were sitting in Kwame's barbershop on Delavan, just south of Grider. I'd gotten my hair cut in Kwame's for years, even before Kwam owned the shop, when it was called "Woody's." I was back home on vacation, sort of, to see family and reminisce. I'd also left Bridgette and A.B., her son. We weren't married, but we were, sort of. Had been living together for three years and been a "couple," whatever that meant to me, for about five. She was 32; I was 47. I loved her fifteen year old son, A.B., but was I in love with her?

"Going to Buffalo," I texted her one day, from work. I'd already packed, but had not told her.

"See you later," was Bridgette's text message back to me.

I didn't go back home that day; I just drove on up to Buffalo from work, after my last class, not telling her a damn thing more, not even "goodbye."

Kwame named the shop The Chessman, because, according to him, "black man's life is like a chess game. War. And I don't want no more casualties. I want brothas to feel that, when they step inside, this is their place, a haven from the battles."

The shop has a chess game motif, with black and red floor tiles and three chess boards, prominently set up for play on one side of the room. Near the boards are customer chairs. In the back of the barber chairs is a counter with a cash register and a mirror. Pictures of black heroes and heroines, Paul Robeson, Malcolm and Martin, and Shirley Chisholm, adorn the shop's walls.

I'd come in for a cut, and we'd got to talking about war, the war facing black men, and chess. The shop was near closing for the night. Only Kwame, the shop owner, Johnny and I were left.

Next thing you know, Johnny started talking about his life, a story he said that was "all about war, man. Straight warfare."

Johnny's Story:

When Delaney left me, she just wrote me a letter and was gone.

Johnny,
The plant called. When you come in you better call them or something. I
told them nothing, so I don't know what they think. Denise and I are gone.
I can't say where. I didn't want to fight, but you know me. Couldn't leave
Nisey, and can't stay here with you.
Be careful,
Delaney

There was nothing in her letter like "I love you," because we didn't say that anymore. I cried and cried. Man, tell you, I cried. Eventually, I had to leave the apartment, and I headed from Stevens toward Delavan, my normal walk to the bus stop at Delavan and Grider. To get to work, I caught the downtown bus, the #13 and then caught another bus over to my job at Republic Steel, on the city's south side. I was scared, because of the killer, but I had my pistol in my lunch pail, just in case. As I walked, I remembered the last time we'd been together as a family, over a week ago now, but my loneliness ached like it was longer.

"Daddy, Momma said for you to git up so you won't be late," my daughter's voice called to me from the other end of the world; really, from the other bedroom in our rented, two-bedroom apartment.

I yelled back, "What'd you say, Nisey? Come here and tell me," because I knew Delaney had told Denise to "come" and wake me; plus, I needed a good morning hug. It might give me the impetus to rise.

"I'm gonna get you up," Nisey said, bounding in the room, jumping on top of me and giggling. "Gimme a horsey ride!" she yelled, but I didn't want to move. Didn't want to leave the comfort of our bed. As usual, Delaney was already up. One while, we slept close, spoon fashion, but now, our bodies refused to touch, even in slumber. Yeah, Laney was up, fixing breakfast as if nothing was wrong, when everything was: there was a crazy, white killer on the loose, killing brothas, and our love was dead, too.

"It's too early, Baby Girl; this horse ain't been fed," I said to Nisey standing in the doorway, facing me. She was posing, hands on her hips, just like her momma.

"Daddy, come on, please, just to the kitchen?"

"OK, Nisey," I sat up. She ran to me, jumping on top, hugging me, and I hoisted her up on my shoulders. She giggled as I stood up, and we galloped into the kitchen.

Her mom and I hadn't really spoken in weeks, or touched in months. Our marriage was dead; we just couldn't bury it. The corpse just lay there, rotting, in the bedroom, and throughout the house. But damn, it didn't smell, probably because Laney had sprayed it with cleanser and wiped it down real good, but the thing was dead for sure.

As we entered the kitchen, Delaney was singing, humming one of those gospel songs they sang in that there church. "Well, the light done come. Can't hide. Can't hide sinner, can't hide," like she was singing about me. One while, I went with them, to keep peace in the house. Laney had said, "I want me a saved man. Head of the household. God's man." But I didn't believe her. She wanted to be the head. So I'd stopped going to church with them.

Now, the marriage was so bad we didn't speak for days. I said to her once, "you speak to God but not with me? That ain't right. God ain't personally getting up and going to the damned plant. That preacher ain't, neither."

I placed our darling down on one of the kitchen chairs and sat across from her at the table. Delaney was standing at the kitchen sink.

"Good morning, Laney," I said to her back. Everything in the kitchen was spick and span, clean white walls, countertops. Hell, you could eat off the black and white tile floor. That woman gave "neat" a new name. But it was all good; that was just her way, but she couldn't handle "my way," the way I was, least that's what I thought.

"John, you and Denise going to eat breakfast or should I toss it?"

"Baby Girl, I think she's mad at us. What you think?"

"I think mommy makes good breakfasts. Let's eat, daddy."

"Yeah, Nisey, let's eat." Reaching for bacon and bread, I wondered if Delaney was thinking about this executioner of brothas. I wasn't afraid to die, just the way they'd been dying, shot in the head, stabbed, the killer creeping up on brothas at bus stops, in their cars, whatever. I wasn't afraid to die, just wanted to fight him, man to man, but he wasn't getting down like that. I didn't want breakfast: bacon and eggs, grits, biscuits, hash browns, juice and coffee. "Thanks for the breakfast, Delaney," I said, because I knew she expected it. I reached for a biscuit, "Laney, I ain't goin' in to work today." Seated beside me at the table, Nisey reached for a biscuit, too, smiling. This was our usual game, Baby Girl imitating me.

"Why, John, why this time?" Delaney turned around from the sink where she was cutting up a chicken, and just stared, like I was an accident she'd drove by and was figuring how the crash had occurred. Then, she just stared, like the car was totaled and there wasn't no use. "Why?" she asked again and her eyes reminded me of how my late momma used to

look when she prayed, searching the sky for God's signal, searching. Well, right now, I was searching, too, but my wife didn't seem to understand.

"Why? .22-Caliber," I said, returning my wife's stare, trying to look behind her eyes, into her heart, her mind.

"That killer ain't studin' you," she said under her breath, like she was telling herself or God, but loud enough for me to hear. I usually ignored her, but not this time.

"Delaney, it ain't safe for a black man in Buffalo these days. And the cops don't care. He just making they job easier, getting rid of some of us for 'em."

"No killer is going to get you, John. You're too hard-headed, rock-headed," she laughed but I thought I heard something else in her voice, a trembling in her voice. I wanted to hear it, a trembling in her voice, a fear for me, for me. Like every time I left, I wanted her to say, "I missed you," when I returned. One while, she used to run and greet me the second I hit the door, but now she was always in bed, asleep, hugging pillows, or up, watching rich, high-talking preachers or soap operas on the tube.

"Naw, baby, that killer ain't gone get me, cause then, he'd have to deal with you, right?" I grinned, looking at my pretty woman, my wife. Laney was 5'6" 140, with glossy, cocoa-brown skin I always wanted to rub, touch, to kiss. I couldn't keep my eyes off her, or my hands, neither, and she knew it. But I had done buried that beneath the ground, and I couldn't dig it up. She wouldn't let me. My pride wouldn't let me. Her eyes always seemed to look beyond me, like there was something, or somebody else, behind me that was more worthy of her attention, even when we were alone, like I was a disappointment she just dealt with. I wanted to get up, put my arms around 'Laney and hug her, hold her tight. But her eyes said "No." Last time in bed that I touched my wife, it was months ago. I had tried caressing her, but there was nothing. It was like I was touching a manikin. So I'd kissed the small of her back and turned to face the bedroom wall. Today, I couldn't do nothing but reach for some more bacon. Baby Girl reached for bacon, too.

"John, you're too crazy to get killed. Bullets bounce off of crazy people, you know," 'Laney said, wiping her hands on her apron, shaking her head.

"If Nisey wasn't here, I'd answer that," I said.

"Go on, answer it anyway. Go on," she said, mad at me for years of messing up. She didn't realize I'd changed. It was like what I did, or didn't do, didn't matter anymore. All that mattered was her judgment and verdict, my conviction.

"Delaney, tell me, what is acting crazy? Tell me, cause I don't know. Naw, never mind, baby. Never mind."

14

"All you know is what, John? What? And don't bother about Nisey being here. She's heard us argue before."

"Well, I ain't trying to argue in front of her." The clock on the kitchen wall ticked like the hands of time. "Maybe I will go to work, after all. What'm I gone do around here, anyway, but get on your nerves? 'Sides, I got something for that killer, come after me." I rose from the table, carrying my dirty dishes to the sink.

"What do you have for the killer, John? Are you going to outrun him? I know you once were a track star, but that was eons ago." She stared at me, as though I were a fool, like I wore a dunce or dummy cap.

"Naw, I got something hard and cold for his honky behind."

"Alright Trouble Man," she said, laughing. But what she didn't know, what I couldn't tell her, was they were talking about closing down my plant, Republic Steel, closing it down. I couldn't tell her that; I hadn't told her that. And all she was thinking about was the man she wanted me to be, the man I couldn't find no more, because he was buried, too.

"Hey, daddy, bring me something home?" Nisey was still at the table, eating biscuits and jelly.

"Nothing to bring, Sweetness, unless you want a bar of steel," I said; I walked over to my child, bent down and began kissing her face.

"Stop, stop Daddy," she giggled. "It tickles, it tickles. You know how your moustache tickles!" But I kept kissing and tickling, kissing and tickling. Laney said nothing. After the tickling, I reached for another biscuit, fast, to see if Nisey followed.

"Okay, Daddy," she said, following my lead, reaching for one, too. "Now, Daddy. When are you going to take me and mommy back to the park and the Buffalo Zoo?"

"I don't know, darling. We'll see."

"You promised you were going to teach me to ride a bike, Daddy, in the park. Delaware Park. You promised."

"Your daddy can't do that right now, Sweetness, but one day, when it's safe again, I will. Promise I will."

"John, there you go again, making promises to her."

"I plan on keeping this one, Laney. She knows I will." I looked at our daughter, then at Delaney. "Swear I will."

"Well, Mr. Serious Man, you best get going, or you won't have a job," Delaney said. Then, she turned to Denise. "Baby, your daddy can't take us to the park right now. He's afraid."

"Yeah, I am afraid." I stood up. "Afraid of what might happen."

Laney laughed. "All that gallavanting you've done, John, and you're afraid of one little white man." She said this out of anger, to get my goat.

We'd already agreed that Nisey could not go anywhere with me. The killer was targeting black men, not little girls, but he might miss.

"Baby, I ain't afraid of nothing but God," I said, staring past her, at the wall behind her, at the black and white curtains that matched the counters and the floors. I stared out the window across the room. And then, I turned to our daughter, "Baby Girl, you know your daddy loves you, right?"

"I know, Nisey said, putting butter and jelly on another biscuit.

I dressed for work, slowly, like if I slowed down, things would change. The killer would be caught, or just disappear. My wife would love me again; we'd be in love. All our bills would be paid. Hell, the Bills would be winners. So far, they were doing good, but I'd learned to never hope too high. I really didn't want to go to work, but it was the only job I had, and what I wanted to do, I couldn't. I had a plan to move down South, where my people had some land in Springfield, Tennessee, near Nashville. About a month ago, I'd showed Laney a newspaper article 'bout how black people need to keep their land, and don't sell it away, to white developers and such, and we ain't had no land here in Buffalo, but Grandpa Wilson had left momma some land in Tennessee, about forty, fifty acres, and I wanted it for us. Maybe it would help our love, give us a new, clean start. There was a shelf in my closet where I kept my gun, beneath our marriage license, birth certificates and my parents' death certificates. I'd been meaning to move it somewhere else. But it was safe here, high enough away from Baby Girl's grasp, in a closet we kept locked. I read the license again, reading the names: "Delaney Deborah Robinson and John Augustus Smith." It hadn't been that long, really, and I still loved that woman. I put the license back in its spot. Then, I reached underneath it for my gun. I packed the gun and some shells in my lunch pail. And I walked out to the living room, thinking that, with a killer running around, this might be my last time. I didn't know.

"Laney," I said, entering the kitchen. She was still at the sink, cutting up that chicken. "Where's Little Bit?"

"Watching cartoons. Her show's on now. *Sesame Street.* You know Nisey doesn't miss that."

"I know. Well, bye, Delaney." I nodded. We didn't hug or kiss anymore, coming or going. I just hoped in my heart she'd be alright, and tried to show it when I looked at her, how I said goodbye.

"Bye, John."

Delaney left me that night. When I got home from work, they was gone. I called around, to her friends and family. Nothing. Nobody was talking. It was like my wife and baby girl had vanished. After that, I didn't go to work for days, calling in sick, hanging out at BB's, the Black Bar, where I felt safe. Hell, I figured, if somebody was gone shoot me, at BB's, least they'd be black. I missed my babies. After three days, I called the cops, but they said wasn't nothing they could do. No evidence of foul play. At first, I thought she'd come back, so I couldn't leave the house, 'cause I needed to be there when they returned. Then I thought, maybe I'd go to work, 'cause she would want me to, and maybe by doing so, God would make her return.

Chapter Two

Barbershop talk—

"Hey, Eddie, man, Kwame asked, why you taking notes, writing all of this down now? Nobody cares, you know. Nobody really cared about the deaths of black men back in 1980, and nobody cares now."

"I care."

"Yeah, but they really don't. Maybe because it was brothers or Buffalo, but nobody cared. And nobody is going to read what you write, if you write about this, man, because they don't care about the deaths of black men, my brotha! Now if it was somebody white, a little white girl, or white women, for real. They at the top of the list, and then white men and boys next. Maybe black women be next, or other people of color. But black men? Naw. Society don't care. They care more about cats and dogs than they do brothas! I dare you, Dr. Researcher. Research that! Here we talkin' bout thirteen dead black men, and nobody knows it happened. How the hell that happen, man? Thirteen black men, men of color murdered, and this killer not be infamous? They ain't made no TV movie bout this here! The dudes that he killed, it's like their lives meant nothing. And now here you are, trying to write about it, something nobody cares about. A serial killer of brothas, in cold-ass Buffalo, NY."

"Yeah," I said, "but shouldn't we care?"

Timeline: September 22, 1980

"Bills Hungry Receivers Return For Seconds," reads the banner above the masthead in The News. The Bills are 3-0, led by Joe Ferguson, Joe Cribbs, and a bunch of black receivers. The headline reads, "Iraqi MiGs Bomb Tehran Airport," and the front page tells how Ronald Reagan is debating John Anderson for the presidency.

One of the first mentions of the killings in the media is a small article in the back of the paper, "Man Sought In Slaying Of Teenager." The article tells of the death of Glenn Dunn, age 14, of Fougeron Street in Buffalo. At about 10 p.m., a hooded gunman begins the killing spree by firing three shots at close range into the head of Dunn, killing him as he sits at the wheel of a stolen car in the Genesee Street parking lot of a Tops Supermarket. According to the article, witnesses saw a man running away from the car moments after the shots. The article also says Dunn came from a loving family, and lived with his grandmother, Vivian Kendrick.

Johnny's story, continued:

The first person I saw when I finally left the house was Rev. Truesome, our next-door neighbor, sweeping trash from his sidewalk into the street, by the curb. Dude was supposed to be connected with some city leaders, big-time preachers and such. I'd called him to ask if he could help me find my family, but no dice.

"Hello Rev. Truesome. You're up pretty early this morning."

Truesome just nodded, like what he was doing demanded total attention. I guessed if the .22-Caliber stepped to him, he was gone sweep the killer to surrender.

Sweeping Through the City was a song Delaney used to sing in that choir one while. This killer was doing that, sweeping black men out the city. I wondered if this was every white man's fantasy, to kill a black man, hurt a brotha. They could hurt you in more ways than one. In Buffalo, they could kill you with promises of jobs, promotions you never got. They could kill you with all the plants closing up, moving out, and then what could you do for a job? How could you feed your family? They could kill you by not allowing you to reach your dream. One while, I dreamed of playing for the Bills: wide receiver. Then, I thought I could play pro basketball, but college never came. I just started working at Republic, and the money was too good to dream anymore. Death could come in a lotta ways, so maybe that was why Truesome was out sweeping his sidewalk. He was fighting death only way he knew how. Hell, I had to figure out how I could fight it, myself. He was bundled up, in a parka and knitted cap, like it was colder out; maybe he knew something I didn't.

"You sure you ain't seen my wife and daughter, know where they at?"

"I already told you, Mr. Smith, I haven't seen them and don't know their whereabouts. I trust they are somewhere safe."

"And where the hell is safe, nowadays, Reverend?" I wanted to clock him, hit him hard, like he was the killer, and I could smash his white ass to oblivion. But he wasn't white. Just a little, old black man with a broom.

"Mr. Smith, I can't answer that. Only God can." His head was bent down toward the ground as he swept, like if he looked down hard enough, maybe the sidewalk held answers.

"Gimme that broom!" I said, and with my free hand, I reached for it.

He jerked back. "What? Mr. Smith. I know you might be upset, but this is my way of . . . "

"Your way of what? Cleaning the damned earth?" I laughed. "Don't you understand man! My wife is gone. My little girl is gone, and this fool is killing us! I can't walk down Stevens and catch the bus without worrying if I'll be shot!"

Now, I had a hold of his broom and I wasn't gone let go. We both held onto it, like we was gone dance. That old man was stronger than I thought. His grip said, "let go." But I couldn't, cause then what? Crazy as it seems, I needed something to hold onto, even a freakin' broomstick.

"J-Smittie, what's goin' on!" Somebody was calling my name. "J-Smittie, man!"

But I kept holding on, like maybe my blessing was in that broom. I looked at the Rev. and I couldn't tell if he wanted to cry or to cuss.

"Johnny Smith!" The sound came from across the street; my name, in a dfferent voice this time. I turned toward the sound: Bubs and Donny Simpkins, blood brothers, were across the street. We played basketball together at the Rec Center on Schuele. I thrust the broom back at Truesome.

"It's yours, Rev.," and ran to greet my friends.

"What's up, Rookies?" We exchanged solidarity handshakes. "Why're y'all so sharp? I know y'all not chasing women this time of day. In their dark suits and white shirts, their shoes shining like clear water, they were dressed like it was Sunday morning, or maybe another funeral.

"Naw, J-Smittie, man. We're goin' up to the Imani House, up on Welker. We trying to get organized."

"I hear ya."

Donny cut in, "Like Kwame always say, it's war, Smittie, man. That's all I got to say. You know where Welker is, just a little north of Jefferson, near Ferry. It's sho nuff war, Smittie."

Three shots, that's all it would take, I thought as we stood talking, there out in the open. Three black men, shooting the breeze like business as usual. Maybe it was: more dead niggas. "Hey y'all, think we should just be standing out here like this?"

"Maybe not," Bubs said.

"Let that killer come my way," Donny said, his face a dark, African mask, a Mandinka warrior's stare.

"He don't just stab, Donald, man, he shoot too. How you gone fight a bullet?" Bubs said.

"Let's walk."

"Later, Rev.," I hollered across the street at Truesome, who'd been watching as he swept the sidewalk, his broom a furious pendulum; swinging it fast, like his life depended on it. Maybe it did; he ignored me.

"Hey y'all, c'mon, let's move," I said, laughing, motioning up the street. I was still thinking about how easy a target we were, huddled on the sidewalk; .22-Caliber could be focusing on us right now.

I can't take this no more, Smittie," Donny said. "I'm ready to kill me some honkies, or mess 'em up real good. Just on principle, man. Eye for an eye, ya know?"

"Man, that's already happening. Did y'all hear about the brothas up on Jefferson Street?

"Naw, Smittie, man, I don't even read the paper no more. Makes me think I'ma die, that I'm gone be next."

"And get this, the police are wondering if it's related to the .22-Caliber. That shooting was the third time this week, according to the paper, that brothas done fired on white people, but there ain't been no deaths, yet."

"I read that, too," Bubs said. "Police said they didn't know whether any of the assaults on whites came in retaliation for the deaths of six blacks."

"Right," I said. "That don't even make sense, man. They got to know it's related."

"Yeah, but we got to start protecting ourselves, fighting back, man."

"We already doing that," Donny said, "an eye for an eye, least we trying to."

"Yeah, we are," I chimed in. "Cause we know it's all related."

"Then you gone join us?" Donny asked.

"Join what?"

"Join our self-defense initiative," he said. "That's why we're going to the Imani."

I'd been to the Imani once or twice; it was a third-floor apartment over a storefront church. One big room and three smaller ones. A group of Rastas and back-to-Africa brothas and sistas who believed in teaching our children, as opposed to sending them to the white man's schools. Malik, one of the brothas who led the group, made African drums and taught poetry.

"We gone fight back," Donny said.

"I think we already are. If the politicians, Mr. Eve and them can't do nothing to stop this mess, then we got to. My wife heard Rev. Anderson and them talking about stay calm. How you gonna stay calm when you might die any second?"

"J-Smittie, man, you got that right. Kadeem gone teach us how to fight back for real, hand-to-hand combat. Kadeem fought in 'Nam. I think you know him."

"Naw, I don't," I said.

"Yeah, you do. Kadeem used to be Benny Williams. Changed his name."

"This killer changing all our names," Bubs said. "Dead black man. That's what he want. Another dead black man."

"Yeah, but this got to stop," Donny said, as they turned to go. "We gone fight this mess, Smittie."

"Yeah," I said, and I wanted to join them, follow them, change my name to Malik, Abdul or whatever, long as my family was safe, I could protect them, and we was together.

"Say hello to the Missus and your baby girl," Bubs added.

"Yeah," I said, 'cause I didn't have the heart to tell them my hearts were gone. As I watched Donald and Bubbles jog up the street, I envied them, and knew they'd fight this fool if they got the chance. I would, too. I had no fear. My heart was gone, so what the hell did I have to fear from a killer who carved out black men's hearts?

I felt so alone. When I woke up now, my covers were wrapped around me like Laney used to be. A car sped by and I thought I heard someone shout, "death to the .22-Caliber," but it could have just been a wish, or the echo of my daydreams.

"Yeah, we gone fight this," I said to myself, as I watched my friends grow smaller as they walked away.

Their dad, Rev. Simpkins, was a pastor. Growing up, our families were close. We lived on Stevens and they lived over on Cambridge, a few streets over. Watching their backs as they walked away, I wanted to run after them. I was at the corner of Carl and Delavan. I caught the bus at the corner of Delavan and Grider. If I caught up to them, what would I say? As I stood on that corner, the wind stung my eyes and water came. I wiped it away and began walking toward my bus stop.

Chapter Three

Barbershop talk—

"This is good," I said to Johnny.

"Why?" Kwame asked, staring at me like he'd been through the whole telling so far.

"Because I wasn't here, Kwam, and this story needs to be told."

"Eddie, man, you really think that it needs to be told, in the new millenium?"

"Yeah, I do."

"Why?"

"O.J., man," Johnny said. "Needs to be told because of O.J. and Malvo and every crazy other black man the media show us. Every infamous black man. They would paint us all like that. When, when . . ."

"When most of us are not crazed maniacs or monsters. We're just invisible," Kwame chimed in, like the brothas in the story, the slain ones."

"You right. They ain't nobody, but they also ain't *nothin'*," Johnny said. "And when Eddie said he was gone use my story in a book, I said, 'naw, ain't nothin' I want to relive, especially read about in some book.' But then, I thought about it, and realized some things need to be told."

"And retold," Kwame added.

"Maybe we can revise history," I said. "This is in none of the history books, you know? Go to the library and look at accounts of mass murderers, and see if you find it."

"I know," Kwame said, "I know. I just wanted to be sure. Run it," he said, grinning, looking up at a photo of Paul Robeson. "His son, Bo, once played wide receiver for the Bills," he said.

I smiled as I looked at Robeson, and I tried to visualize him, or someone who looked like him, running out in the open for a touchdown pass. "You sure that was his son?"

"Naw," Kwame said, "I ain't sure."

"What the heck," Johnny says. "They still probably kin."

"Yeah!" I shouted. "Let's run with it. Let's run!"

We laughed.

But that night, I didn't laugh. I prayed and I cried. Talked with Bridgette, because I felt guilty that I hadn't called, as if I had deserted her. But I was paying the bills and they stayed in my house. My house. She

didn't ask, "Why haven't you called," or "When you coming home," as though perhaps she expected me to offer. Or maybe she was content with my being away. We spoke about Anderson, her son, the closest I would ever come to having my own son. Since we'd started dating, I had taken him with me everywhere, basketball outings, ball games, and Buffalo. We were running buddies.

"He misses you," she said. "Sits in that old car you gave him and plays his trumpet. When I asked 'why,' he said, 'So Eddie and I can jam when he gets back.' But I didn't have the heart to tell him you're gone indefinitely, Ed."

"I'm coming back," I said. "Working on my manuscript," I mumbled, because we both knew the manuscript was just an excuse, or another reason, to stay away.

"I know what you're working on, Ed. I've got to go. Got work in the morning. Bye."

"Bye." In the silence, I wondered, how could I leave her for good, when I'd left her, already, in so many ways? Once, after we'd argued, I'd said, "When we make love, I feel like I'm with the slave master's woman, his concubine."

"You're been reading too many books," she said. "Our lives are not *Roots*.

Another time, I asked her, "So, did he rape you, the white dude, Anderson's daddy?"

"I don't know."

"Right."

"Eddie, I was drunk. I used to party hard. So, do you hate me because I've been with white men?"

"How many?"

"What?"

"How many?"

"Why? Why the hell are you asking that?"

"Maybe there's a cut-off point, or something, a tipping point, when I say, 'that's too many white boys,'" I laughed. She didn't.

Timeline: Tues. September 23, 1980

At about 12:30 p.m., Harold Green, age 32, another black man, an industrial engineer, is shot while he sits in his car, eating lunch at a fast food restaurant on Union Road in Cheektowaga, a suburb of Buffalo. The gunman, wearing a blue golf hat, reaches into the open car window and fires two shots into Green's head. Green does not die immediately and is under 24-hour guard at St. Joseph's Hospital.

Later that day, at about 11:30 p.m., the killer strikes again, shooting Emmanuel Thomas, age 30. According to witnesses, Thomas is talking with a friend at 11:30 p.m. at the corner of East Ferry and Zenner, when his wife calls to him from the window of their apartment at 70 Zenner Street. Thomas, an unemployed waiter, and father of two young children, begins crossing the street but is blocked by traffic.

A white gunman approaches Thomas from the rear, screaming "Hey, you," and fires three shots from close range, hitting him once in the skull.

Thomas is pronounced dead on arrival at Erie County Medical Center (ECMC).

Police term the killings execution-style shootings and begin searching for a motive. The story is now front-page news in the local papers: *Pedestrian Shot to Death on the East Side* and *Two More Executed; Police Look for Link.* There is also a story about how the police see a link between the two parking-lot shootings. But there is no mention, yet, of race, of black skin being a link.

The Iraq-Iran war is still big in the news, and the city has a new slogan, *Buffalo, We're Talking Proud!*

Johnny's Story, continued:

I had options. I could go home and sit, feel sorry for myself, or I could join my friends at the Imani, maybe try to help my community cope. As I thought about the dead, I wished I knew them. Wished I could have helped stopped the killing. What Delaney didn't understand was, I couldn't let this happen and not do something. Wasn't that why Martin Luther King had died? So the black man could be a man? Wasn't that why Shirley Chisholm had run for president? So black people could have a voice? Standing out in the cold, I shivered, thinking that my voice was gone, blown away by cold wind coming down from Canada. I pulled up my collar, wondering if the men had cried out or shouted when they died. I wondered if our love was dead. I wanted Delaney, but then I didn't, since I couldn't give her the man she wanted.

Y'all might remember Fred Smith, manager of the gas station on the corner of Delavan and Grider; well, that was across from where I caught my bus. We joked all the time about being kinfolks; we weren't, just friends, but he was crazy about our little Nisey, called her his little grandniece. Figured I'd shoot the bull with Fred while waiting for the bus.

"Cousin, you look preoccupied, man," Fred said when I reached his station.

"My wife gone," I said.

"She be back. That woman love you, Cat. Y'all joined at the hearts," he said, wiping a window of the station.

"I thought so, but I don't know no more." The wind blew, stinging my eyes, and water came. I turned so Fred couldn't see my face. "I'm scared man."

"Ain't no killer gone come around here," Fred said, "long as I got Freeda with me." He jerked his head back toward the store behind the counter where he kept his shotgun.

"I'm scared she ain't coming back, Fred. Scared my baby girl will forget her daddy. Scared he might find them."

"Dude, he ain't killing nobody but *us*. Black cats, like maybe we done something to him, that make only us the targets. Maybe he with the KKK or something. You heard how they acted up at that boy, Dunn's funeral. Now, that's just disrespectful. White people. This might be 1980, but in some people heads, we still in 1955.

"Yeah."

"Now that was right in the heart of the community, Black man, like they just gone come on in and rub it in our faces."

"Like they killing us in our faces, Fred."

"I know. But your family gone be alright, Johnny. You got you a good woman. And she ain't just gone leave you like that."

"I hope not, man. Well, I best be getting on over to that bus stop if I'm going to work." We exchanged soul handshakes.

"Alright, Brotha Smittie," he said, flashing the black power sign.

"But hey, Fred, man, when you gone sell me that car?" I asked, pointing to an old Buick deuce and a quarter that sat in a corner of his lot.

"Have your Missus come and talk with me about it. I trust her more than I do your ass," he laughed.

I waved him off and started toward the bus stop. As I walked, I remembered a talk I'd had with my baby girl.

"Daddy, I'm scared," Nisey said one night as I was reading bedtime stories, *Gingerbread Man* and the *The Sky is Falling*, her favorites. I'd read 'em to her umpteen times, but she always wanted to hear these stories, not some others. Laney liked me to tuck in Nisey when I could.

"The first and last voices she hears every day should be ours, Johnny. I'll wake her up and you tuck her in when you're home."

At first, I didn't want to, but then, it became our special time.

"I'm scared daddy. I don't want to go to school no more."

"Why, Sweetness?"

"You know."

"I do?"

"Yeah, you and Mommy think I don't know. But I'm a big girl and I know things."

"Okay, baby, I understand, but you don't have to worry. The killer ain't, I mean, isn't, going after little girls, just grown black men, like me."

I pulled her closer as we sat side-by-side at the head of her bed; I kissed her forehead.

"But what if he changes his mind, daddy?"

"I'll never let anybody hurt my baby girl, ever. To get to you, they gotta come through me. That's a daddy's job, Sweetness."

"Or mommy, too?"

"Yes, 'or mommy too,'" I said.

Now they were gone, and I couldn't save them, shield them. Maybe it was just an extended leave. Maybe Delaney felt Nisey would be better, safer, if she wasn't around me. I had stopped taking Nisey anywhere with me outside. The risk was too great, that the killer, in trying to kill me, might hit her. How could a black man save his daughter, when he endangered her with his presence? I didn't know. All I knew as I stood on the corner, peering down Grider, looking for the bus, was that I missed my family and wanted them back. I had to get them back, and I didn't care how.

Chapter Four

Barbershop talk—

"Winter always comes early in Buffalo," Johnny said, "and here I was looking forward to the Bills' season that year."

"We always looking forward to their season," Kwame said, "and then what?"

"Yeah, we been used to losing, even before the Bills did so four straight times, in the biggest game of all," Johnny said.

"When I read about the victims, I wondered if I knew any of them, or knew people who knew them. Y'all know I didn't come back home a lot back then."

"You probably did, Eddie, man." Kwame said. "We all kin, you know."

I laughed, to hide my guilt at abandoning home at some point, in pursuit of something I still didn't have. I guessed I thought writing this would help me achieve it, but I couldn't tell them that, so I laughed. I laughed because I didn't want to lose this here, brothas sharing, talking. Black men, sharing, bonded by race and class, generation and locale. I laughed, because I had been crying inside for so, so, long. These men were my brothers, or else, I had none. I wondered if they knew that, why I had to take down Johnny's story, their story, try to make it mine.

Just like Bridgette was my woman, or I was womanless. But how could she be my woman, when I loathed what she represented?

"Why'd you name him 'Anderson Black Anderson?'"

"I was so alone, Eddie. I had hid my pregnancy from everybody for six months. And I had A.B. during my seventh month. Nobody really knew, except my best friend, Deanna. I was in that hospital, thinking, and I'm not sure what they asked me, but I guess my answer was 'Anderson.' I put the 'Black' in to be militant," she said softly, "to let them know, he was black. To let him know, too."

"Even though the world's gonna let him know?"

"Yes."

"Even though he has an unknown white daddy?"

"Yes. But not 'unknown,' I guess I could find him if I wanted to, if I tried."

"What was his name?

"Karl," she said.

"Karl? What's his last name, what's the rest?"

"Karl-you-know-I-don't-know-the rest," she said, staring at me, her eyes sleepy, dreamy, as though this wasn't real, just a scene in a flick.

"Why don't you know?" and I hated us both, right then.

Bridgette Alicia Anderson, my 32-year old fiancé, whom I knew I'd never marry, but never, ever leave, either. Here we were, stuck in slow-ass Fairborn, Ohio, living together, or doing whatever the hell we were doing. I was a middle-aged professor at a local college, struggling to write my tenure book. Struggling to stay with Bridgette. I struggled to leave her, too.

They'd moved in after our second year together. She had been living with her aunt and cousins, while working at a local grocery store, as assistant manager.

"So you named him Black, so people would know he was black, huh?"

"Shut up."

"He's white, too, you know."

"And so are you, you Oreo. You may think 'black,' but you live 'white.' Those black books you teach separate you from real black people, you moron."

"Naw, you separate me," I laughed.

Bridgette was light-skinned, what some black folks called a "red-bone." I hated that phrase. Anderson, at first glance, could pass for white. He was very light; well, he was white, really, or, white-pink, with straight auburn hair. And blue-green eyes. She said she'd had eyes that color when young but they'd changed.

"Maybe it would be good if his changed, too."

"Why? I think it's adorable, adds to his charm."

"Might add to getting his behind kicked, too, in the hood. He'd look less 'white' if they changed."

"Are you jealous?"

I didn't answer her, just walked away.

But at 15, he was 6'3" and growing, with a wide receiver's build, broad shoulders, big hands. I figured if he had handles, he'd make a good point or two-guard. The kid, though she coddled him, could play some ball. The five years I had been with his momma, I'd tried to make him into the ball player I'd never been, maybe even the brotha, the black man I never was. I'd kicked his behind, until he could beat me with ease; then, I'd taken him to gyms where we'd run ball with street ballers and thugs, ex-college and high school players, some of them former students of mine, and he held his own.

I told them, "be hard on his ass."

Timeline: September 24, 1980

The 36-hour series of attacks moves to Niagara Falls, NY, where the killer, holding the gun in a brown paper bag, shoots Joseph McCoy, age 43, as McCoy walks down the street. The blond youth who walks up behind him, puts his arm around McCoy's shoulder and fires two shots as McCoy walks down 11th Street in the Falls.

The Same Gun Used To Shoot 3 Victims, the headline proclaims. And now, the police have a composite sketch. According to Police Chief Leo Donovan, the killer is a white male, 30 to 35 years old, 5 feet, 10 inches tall, with a chubby face and a pale complexion. The police plan on hypnotizing the lone witness in the Harold Green shooting, in hopes of getting a better description of the gunman.

In what the news calls "related incidents," a young white man is stopped by a group of blacks in the Falls as he walks, carrying a paper bag from which a black handle protrudes. The group holds him, thinking he might be the killer. Police and detectives free the man after finding he was merely carrying a hacksaw he'd just bought.

Also, the life of a black bus driver is threatened, and seven detectives are assigned to provide him with protection, riding not only on his bus but also in squad cars as escorts. The iceberg tip of hysteria has just been revealed.

The papers also reports on a Buffalo police slowdown, in a wage dispute. Throughout the killing spree, this slowdown enrages the black community, giving rise to its fears of genocide, rise to rumors of a conspiracy to kill black men.

Johnny's Story, continued:

As I was looking down the street for the bus, I heard a car horn. It was from a car stopped at the red light. The passenger window rolled down, and a white man called me, "Hey, John, John Smith!" This white man I didn't know was calling my name. I stepped back, raising my lunch pail to my heart.

"Hey, John, John Smith. John, you need a ride?" He was leaning across the passenger's seat from the driver's side, straining to make me know him, recognize his face, but all I thought about was pulling out my gun.

"Smittie," he said, his face red and concerned, "Going my way? It's Bill, Bill Reilly." He smiled as he said this, like he was a friend.

I was ready to put a cap in him right then and there. Kill or be killed. I looked up and down the street, reached in my pail for my gun.

"Delaney's teacher!" he shouted at me.

Then, I remembered. Bill Reilly. Yeah, he was Delaney's teacher at the community college. I got to know him because he called her his "star student;" she'd even won some college award he'd nominated her for.

"Naw," I said, waving him off. "I don't need no ride. No thanks, man," . . . but then I thought I shouldn't wait for that bus. It would be safer in this white man's car; besides, I'd get to work sooner. I ran to his car before the light, or his mind, changed.

"Thanks," I said, getting in. It was some sort of green foreign car, like a Volvo, Audi, or V-dub. Not flashy, but classy, nice, with a stick shift and black leather seats.

"You're on your way to where?" he asked, his eyes focusing on the road as the light changed.

"Work. Thanks," I said again, unsure what else to say.

"Republic Steel, right?"

"You got a good memory."

"Yeah, I try to keep up with my students' lives, including my former students. And your wife was one of my best students."

"What classes she take from you?"

"A couple, *Humanities 101: Introduction to Great Books*, and then also *Creative Writing: The Memoir*. She ace'd both classes. A real deep thinker, your lady. You must be proud of her."

"Yeah," I said.

"So how's Delaney doing? My colleagues and I always encouraged her to get her Bachelor's and maybe more. She was that perceptive and insightful."

I couldn't tell him that she was gone, but I wanted him to continue, because his words might give me a clue. I couldn't tell him how we'd fought over her schooling. How I'd said, "I don't want you to get ahead of me, Laney. I'm afraid that when you get your degrees and all, you won't want me." Maybe she was leaving me for a college guy or to finally finish that degree. After Denise had been born, she'd had to stop school, because who was going to care for our daughter? And sometimes, we needed Laney to work, too, temp stuff, since she had accounting and typing skills. Plus, it was easier for her to get and keep a good job than me.

"Laney's fine," I said. "Fine. She still reads a lot."

"Well, that's one fine lady you have. And your little girl, she must be getting big now." He was driving north on Ferry Street, like he was going to take me all the way to work, but I wasn't sure I wanted to go.

"Yeah, Nisey is five now, just started kindergarten." I remembered how, after Denise had been born, he'd come to the christening, at Deliverance

34

Church. Everybody had made a big fuss over him and his date, whoever she was. White people, a college teacher, showing up at the event, for a black baby dedication. They'd given us a gift for our baby, and afterward, he'd held Denise in his arms. I'd wondered then, if she was the first black baby he'd ever touched or held. Probably. "Right now, I can't stand white people. Hate y'all," I said, staring at him. His face turned beet red as he focused on the road.

"John. I'll tell you something." He continued focusing on the road. I wasn't sure if he was scared of me, or just intent on driving. I wanted to scare his ass. "Right now, I can't stand them either, white people. So, you want me to drive you all the way to work, or drop you off somewhere?"

"I want to kill the white cat who is killing us. I got a gun," I said. His face turned white, then red, then white again. Guessed he thought he was trying to do a good deed, and now he was in the car with a crazy-ass nigga. Hell, I just wanted him to feel what I was feeling, what we were feeling. His hands trembled at the wheel. I was glad. I wanted to make this man shake with fear in his own car.

But he spoke, even louder, above the music on the car stereo. "I don't blame you, John," he said. "I want him dead, too. And I'm a pacifist. Anyhow, whoever he is, he needs to be put away, for a long time. These killings are making me rethink my stand on the death penalty. I know you might not believe this but a lot of whites are sick over these killings, too. My college department held a meeting recently, during which we discussed what we could do, what kind of statement we could make, in light of this spree."

As I looked at this white man, I realized that, for the first time in my life, I wanted somebody dead: the killer. Or maybe I just wanted somebody white dead. "Help me find him, Bill." I looked at the road in front of us. I gripped my lunch pail tighter to my chest. "Help me find them."

"John, your guess is as good as mine, and who knows where he'll strike next."

Now, Earth, Wind and Fire was playing on the stereo. "Laney loves this tune," I said. "Shining Star."

"Yes, I know," he said. He said it like he knew my wife, like they were more than just teacher and student.

I wanted to punch him. "You *know?*" We were stopped at a light, and I wanted to punch him. I wanted to hurt this friendly white man, take his money, cuss him the hell out, something, anything, to make him pay. Make them pay for my stomach being in knots and my sleepless nights. "What you mean, 'you know'"?

"I know, because my students write about their loves and passions."

"Help me find them," I said, thinking of how I had made a tape with this same music on it, a copy of one I'd made for her a few months ago. Laney had said it was so nice, smooth soul songs, that she wanted to give one to a friend. So this peckerwood was that "friend." I was burning.

"You said that before. Who, John? Who are they?"

"My wife, my daughter. They're gone, afraid of the killer," I lied. "She left a note saying she couldn't stay in Buffalo. I think she's gone to Canada." Saying that, I thought of the Peace Bridge, spanning the lake and uniting Canada and the USA. Maybe that's where she went, or where I needed to go. "Drop me off at the Peace Bridge," I said. "I think she went to the Falls, or maybe up to Toronto."

"My favorite city," he said. "Let's talk about this, Johnny." He was turning left on Fillmore, and I wondered if I should tell him to let me off here, since the Fillmore bus would take me to work, but I really didn't know if I was going.

"Nothing to talk about, Bill. Either you want to help me, or you don't, understand?" I focused on the grey-ness outside: grey building, grey fall trees, grey sky.

"Yes, okay, but I still need to understand what you need from me."

"I already told you. Your help."

"Let's discuss this," he said. He pulled the car into a church parking lot near Humbolt and High streets. "You need my help. What kind of help?" It was near Rev. Simpkins's church, Bubs and Donnie's father. He parked the car.

"White man kind. The type only you or your kind can give me."

"My kind? If we had more time, I'd ask what you mean by that last comment, 'my kind,'" he said, letting the motor run. He turned down the radio. "John, I don't know what's going on with your family, but I do know this, Delaney talked nonstop about you. And once that little girl was born, I remember you three at the christening. Is this the church?"

"No."

"I remember how you looked, content, happy. Your face reflected the light in Delaney's, like the two of you and that baby were the only people in the world at that moment. The rest of us were spectators, but the three of you were insulated by love, as if there was there was a glass bubble in which you dwelt. Watching, I was envious."

"You, envious, of me? Here you a white guy with money and a doctor's degree? A college teacher, I mean, professor, and you envy me?"

"Admire, then. I admired you your family. The unity and love. It's what EWF sings about, you know?" He said, smiling as though telling me a secret. "Love, unity, utopia. That's what EWF sings about, a land where

dreams can be realized. And I have to thank Delaney for that. That's why, when I was at the christening, I said to myself, Billy Reilly, now this kind of love is where it's at. This is exactly where it's at."

"Utopia? Define 'utopia' for me."

"Utopia is a special concept, a sense of a perfect place, a perfect space in time, perhaps just a moment, even. Does that help define it for you?" He looked at me as though I was his student. Maybe he was a good guy, a good white cat, but I couldn't believe that right now.

"Yeah, you did a good job. But this here's my utopia." I pulled the gun out of my lunch pail. "Get out, Doc."

"Huh? What are you doing, John? I don't understand."

"And you won't. You never will. Just get out. I'm not playing." I poked the pistol in his side; his body twitched. "I need your car."

His face was red. His eyes watered up. He gripped the steering wheel like he wouldn't let go. "The whole world's gone crazy. There's insanity all around, but I can't let us become part of it. I wanted to help you." His voice rose, falsetto. "I picked you up because it was my way, my gesture, of trying to counter the current racial madness. John, just tell me where you need to go, and I will drive you around, but . . . "

"You damn straight it's all crazy. Those white people came down to that boy's funeral to poke fun! What's that about? I'm tired of all of y'all. I'm sorry, man, but I just need this here car right now."

"Yes, I know what's going on. I've been keeping up with everything," his voice rose, his red face glistened, moist.

"Do you? Do you really?"

"Well, I'm trying. I'm really trying. You can ask your wife."

"What do you mean, ask my wife? What can she tell me that you can't say, right here, right now?"

"All I mean is, whatever is going on, John, it doesn't give you the right to hijack my car."

"Call it hijacking if you want. I call it borrowing, and if you don't give me this car, I'm gone shoot your ass. I swear I will." I cocked the gun. "Get out, Bill Reilly."

"You really mean this, don't' you?" He took his hands off the steering wheel, as though he might try something. I prayed he wouldn't.

"Get out and get to stepping, man," I poked his ribs with the gun again. "I'm one second from using this thing." I was bluffing him. I slapped his head with my free hand. "Get out, man. Now."

He looked at me, his mouth open like betrayal. "Can't you at least drive me home?"

"Where, man? Where?"

"Sweet Home Road, Amherst," he was unlocking the door.

"That's white folks' territory. I don't go into white folks' land unless I have to anymore. They shoot blackies out there."

"So I'm just going to have to walk?" He was getting out of the car.

"Yeah. You white. You be alright. Ain't nobody hunting your ass like they are mine." I slid over to the driver's side and looked up at him, standing outside his car. "You'll be alright," I said, "and if you're not, it's payback. Since you know so much about black music, I know you 'member "The Big Payback. James Brown." I revved the engine. "I need your ride more than you do. Sorry, Charley," I laughed and slammed the door shut, hard. He jumping, backing away like I was gone shoot him. "See ya, Sweet Homes," I said.

"Alright, John," he said, looking around, like help was coming. "So, is that all you want from me? May I go now?"

"I ain't no thief. I'll return your car when I find my woman. But right now, I gotta take what I need, in order to find my family."

"I'm in the phone book," he said, backing up, facing me, as though I might shoot him in the back, like he couldn't just turn and walk away. But I had what I needed, his car. "William J. Reilly, on Sweet Home in Amherst."

"I got it, Sweet Homes. Besides, I'm sure my wife knows it," I said, wanting him to catch my drift. "I'll ask Laney to help me find it." I stared at him as I said her name, 'cause I wanted to see something in his face that would tell me to pop this dude. I wanted to hurt him, like he and his kind were hurting me. I wanted to be able to go home to my wife, her food, her orderliness, and Baby Girl's giggles and squeals: "Daddy, daddy!" "Get out my face, man," I said.

"Okay," and then Bill turned and began walking away, south, in the direction of Fillmore Ave. Watching the slightly built, hippy-dressed white guy slowly walk away, probably toward a bus stop, I prayed he'd be okay. Hell, he was white. He'd be alright.

Chapter Five

Barbershop talk—

"I'm tired, Kwam, Eddie. Let's quit for the night, okay? Pick it up tomorrow."

"Okay, kool."

"Tomorrow it is," I said. "But remember, I go back to Ohio next week, and I need this story to complete my book."

"My story," Johnny said. "My story. Remember that."

"What do you mean? Now, you don't want me to have it?"

"Naw, I do, but it's bigger than that," he said, rising, reaching toward the ceiling. "Gets to a point where the people who know your story, some of them dead or not in your life no more, so the story you carry is the only connection you got left with 'em."

"Yeah, I hear ya," I said, rising, more tired than I'd realized. The darkness outside invited us all to take a break, and I was ready to leave.

"That's how I feel, Eddie, man. It's theirs, but it's mine, like my dead friends' stories done walked into mine, so mine is heavier now."

"What did you do to my son?" she screamed into the phone.

"Nothing, Bridgette, nothing. Calm down."

"Don't you tell me to calm down, and don't say 'nothing,' when you get on the phone saying that my baby, my son, is in the Emergency at the hospital. What happened, Eddie? What the hell happened?"

"We were playing ball, at the Rec, and they knocked him down."

"What do you mean, 'they knocked him down?' I trust you with my son, you can take him anywhere you want with you and then you let him get mugged. And he thinks you're some kind of god, and then you go and get him hurt? You did this to get at me, didn't you, Eddie? Didn't you? You know I don't trust you anymore."

"He was going up for a dunk, and a couple of cats clothes-lined him. Knocked him down, hard, so he wouldn't embarrass them. Told him about embarrassing black cats down in the hood."

"I'm on my way, but I don't trust you anymore. I don't. You did this to me, too."

I wanted to tell her it was part of the game, and that the cats thought he was white and showing off, and that he'd be a better player in the long run for it. Shit, he'd be a white secret weapon. College coaches were always looking for white cats who could ball like brothers and here was

one who was a brother but could pass for white. They could play him and still meet their quota of white boys on the court.

"Where is he now? Eddie, did you hear anything I just asked you? Where is Anderson, now?"

Her words pulled me back. "The doctor is looking at him, I think. I'm in the waiting room."

She hung up the phone. Turned out, he'd broken his forearm, as he'd tried to break his fall, as he went flying. Dude had taken off from just inside the foul line, on a break-away dunk, and they'd met at his body, two O.G.'s, old-time ballers who wanted to teach a young blood a lesson.

"Damn', man, why'd you do that?" I asked him as we drove to the hospital. His eyes were bloodshot, he was holding his left arm like it was broken. And he'd had to be carried to my car by me and Josh, an old friend who still played ball, too.

"Told you I could dunk on anyone," he winced a confident grin.

"But you can't," I said. "Sometimes you can't fly, man."

She slapped me.

"Don't you ever, ever, ever, hurt my son, again. I will kill you, you no-good, self-centered, arrogant bastard." She was crying and yelling in my face. I'd stood when I spied her running down the hospital corridor toward me, to greet her. And now she was in my face, talking loud enough that the entire waiting room was staring. "You're supposed to be taking care of him, watching out for him, and this happens? Take me to my son. Where is he?"

She left me for the counter. I stood and watched as they led her back to him.

I wanted to join her, to go back with her to see about him, as a family, but she let me know time and again that we weren't. It was three separate couples: she and I; he and I; and the two of them. They were family, I wasn't. Like the time I chastised him, and he lied, saying I'd choked him, when all I'd done was grab him by the shoulders and say, "don't steal," and "don't let me catch you going into stores taking things that don't belong to you." This had been during our first year together, and I had a hard grip, but I hadn't tried to hurt the little dude, just let him know that when I took him out, he couldn't be trying to cop a five-finger discount. "Especially since people are going to wonder why a tall black man has a little white boy stealing for him. So, no, you can't be stealing when you're with me. Because they will lock my ass up, not yours!"

Timeline: Saturday, September 27, 1980

Today is the funeral of the 14-year-old, Glenn Dunn. Ray Hill, a white local news columnist, attends the service and writes an impassioned piece on it: *Revenge is the Lord's*. But some at the funeral speak of taking revenge themselves. They speak of arming themselves in order to fight this unknown assassin. The small sanctified church can't hold the hundreds who have come to offer their sympathy, condolences to his family, father, mother and grandmother. When the pews fill up, they sit in folding chairs, and they stand in the aisles. The church sings, *I'm Going on a Long Journey*, and the preachers preach about *God's inscrutable will*.

The words of the reporter, Hill, are eloquent, as he, recalls how "Dunn, a black boy, once in the church Sunshine Band, was now dead." I'd been in the Sunshine Band, too. And I wondered what the killer saw, or didn't see, to compel him to kill the kid.

One of the first of many racial incidents to result from the shootings occurs outside Dunn's funeral. During the service, two cars of white youths pull up outside the church and begin taunting blacks entering the church, attending the funeral. The white hecklers had painted their faces and bodies red and drawn bullet holes on their faces. The head of a mannequin smeared with a red, blood-like substance, is perched on a fender of one of their cars, presumably in mockery of the dead child. Further, according to witnesses, the whites follow the funeral procession on its route, taunting, heckling, and jeering at the mourners.

Sunday, September 28, 1980

Harold Green, who was actually the second victim shot, dies today.

Today, uniformed police guard the guests at the Black Achievers Banquet held at the Statler Hotel. More than 1,600 turn out at the hotel to honor twenty-six people at the 8th Annual Black Achievers Dinner. More than 300 persons are turned away because there's no room for them. Mayor Griffin, County Executive Rutkowski and other local leaders attend. Blacks in attendance know that the numbers who came and the appearance of the dignitaries are at least partially due to the killer, signs of solidarity on the one hand and political expediency on the other. City Councilman Herbert Bellamy, addressing the gathering, says, "This is the answer to a lot of Buffalo's problems—people pulling together."

The Bills win again today, and are 4-0, but people in the city wonder when the bubble's going to burst.

Johnny's Story, continued:

I slid over to the driver's seat in Bill Reilly's car, and switched the radio to the news. The newsperson said, "The manhunt for the crazed killer known as the .22-caliber killer has polarized the city. Racial animosity has reached an-all time high in Buffalo. Local Black leaders are calling for a boycott and a rally." I switched to other stations. Some of them played music. Others played news. It was all the same, really. Craziness in Iran, with the hostages. Craziness here in Buffalo with the killings. Craziness in my home. What home? I decided to find and follow Bill, at a distance. Maybe he would lead me to my woman. Maybe he was the .22-Caliber. Probably not. But maybe, just maybe, this white man knew where my wife and daughter were. If he did, I'd kill him.

Timeline:

Monday, September 29, 1980
All four men died from bullet wounds from the same gun. All four were shot on the left of the head. The papers run editorials calling the apprehension of the killer the *highest priority* and an *urgent task for police*. The Buffalo Police rule out the possibility that Joseph Paul Franklin, wanted for questioning in the shooting of National Urban League president, Vernon Jordan, and other blacks in five cities, is a suspect in Buffalo.

Investigators from Buffalo, Niagara Falls, and Cheektowaga, all three communities where the slayings occurred, have hit a dead end, in spite of hundreds of tips and clues. Moreover, the longer the killing spree continues, the more tense the situation will become, according to the Rev. Bennett Smith, local coordinator of Operation PUSH. Rev. Smith also expresses concern that the FBI isn't involved yet, stating, "It would be a simple matter for a case to be made for civil rights being violated." PUSH begins raising reward money.

Tuesday, September 30, 1980
The reward begins to grow from different sources throughout the city, from both the black and white communities, as well as local businesses: a $1,000 reward is put up by The Buffalo News and WKBW TV for information leading to the arrest and conviction of the killer.

Wednesday, October 1, 1980
The FBI enters the investigation because, according to U.S. Attorney, Richard J. Acara, the civil rights of two of the victims *may have been*

violated because the killer interfered with their right to public accommodations. One was shot in a restaurant and one in a supermarket parking lot. The locales of the shootings allow the authorities to use the old Civil Rights legislation, from the sit-ins, to bring the Feds into the case. This legislation links the Buffalo violence to the 60's struggles when blacks in the South integrated lunch counters, soda fountains and any other facility *which serves the public and is principally engaged in selling food and beverages.*

For Buffalo blacks, walking on the street, eating a hamburger and fries, have become gestures of courage, acts against fear and paranoia which link the city with the struggles of the past, when young blacks sat down at lunch counters knowing they would be beaten, spat upon, jailed. Now, we knew we might die just for being black.

According to the police, a white man in a neighborhood where one of the shootings happened said to a black woman, *You're next* or *You're going to get it* and then fled. But no black women have been shot, just brothers.

By this point in the investigation, the police have gotten over 200 calls and tips, including one from a man who identified himself as the killer. And there's another where, according to the media, a wife called the cops to say she thought her husband was the killer, but she refused to give his identity.

Thursday, October 2, 1980
Police officials from the Niagara Frontier, Buffalo, Niagara Falls and Cheektowaga meet in an attempt *to reassure the black community that the investigation had been a coordinated effort from the beginning.*

But the black community is not assured, and continues to wonder if it would have been different if brothers weren't the only victims.

Johnny's Story, continued:

I drove in the exact direction Riley had walked, toward the bus stop at Bailey and and East Utica. I figured he'd take the Bailey out to the suburbs.

I drove south down Utica, toward Fillmore. I crossed over Fillmore, thinking maybe I'd just search through the streets of the city, looking for him, looking for them, my family. He couldn't have gotten very far, walking. But I didn't see him at any bus stops. I switched the dial as I drove, hoping to find the right station, one that would give me some clues. I drove slowly, hoping I'd see them at any moment, or like the killer was around the corner. I stopped the radio on a station that was playing some Michael Jackson: *Rock With You.* I laughed, recalling how Nisey and I

would put on a show for Laney, each of us with a white glove on one hand, Baby Girl and me singing with Michael and moonwalking. She'd sing, *Rock with me, daddy,* and I'd moonwalk around the kitchen table, while Laney would stand at the sink or the stove, as always, shaking her head at us. Damn, I missed those days. Rain-sleet was falling, so I couldn't see as clearly as I would like to, but what was I looking for? Delaney? Reilly? The killer? I didn't know, guess I'd know who I was looking for when I found 'em.

I saw a crowd, ten, fifteen people in a circle on a vacant lot, beside some boarded-up buildings.

"What's up?" I parked across the street from one of the buildings. It had a bunch of church revival signs posted on it, so you couldn't see no building, no wood, just signs.

One of the signs I could make out from the car: *Souls Saved. Bodies Healed. Signs And Miracles.*

I needed a miracle. I rolled down the windows of the car and looked into the dark crowd. Music was blasting, like it was a party, or something, and people was shouting. But they wasn't party shouts, more like yells and screams, so I got out the car, careful to look around, careful to take my pail with me. People, on both sides of the street, standing by, staring at the circle, with the hollers and screams coming from inside that circle.

Crossing the street, walking toward the crowd, I made out shouts, "Get his ass. Stomp him to death. Kill that mofo!"

Mingled with the shouts were cries of, "Help! Help!"

After crossing the street, I stood back, behind the crowd, and got my gun out my pail, careful so no one saw. The rain-sleet mess was coming down harder now. It was that usual Buffalo, cold rain-sleet like we were gone have another snow storm in October. Somebody was on the ground, surrounded by the circle. The body on the ground was punched, kicked, hit, with fists and feet and wooden boards and baseball bats. They stomped on that body like they were dancing, and it was the dance floor: *Rock With Me.* They stomped, and I just stood and stared. It was a dude's body. It was a white man. Surrounded by a group of young, hungry black men, beating him, stomping his ass into the ground. I approached slowly, to see better. They stomped and laughed and cussed his ass into the ground. I moved even closer, amazed none of them acknowledged my presence. Maybe they didn't care; maybe I was invisible to them. Maybe this poor white man was all they saw.

It was Bill Reilly.

"Oh no," 'cause it was like Bill Reilly was meat and they was all taking bites. They was cursing, kicking him, and laughing. Each dude who kicked him, kicked him into somebody else's foot, until another foot kicked his

ass across the circle. Like he was a log on the ground. And when he tried to get up, they kicked him back down. They didn't care where they kicked him, in the face, the head, wherever.

I walked closer. "God help me," I prayed. "Help me," and I shot in the air.

"Y'all get off him now! Now! Y'all, move!"

Nobody did nothing, like they didn't hear or care. I stepped closer. I shot again, this time on the ground, just outside the circle.

"Y'all move!" I shouted, and some of 'em turned around.

"What the . . ." " one of 'em said.

"I said, move offa his ass. Leave him be." My stomach was hurtin', like somebody fists was punching my gut, but I kept my voice low, deep-like, like I was they boss. Like me and my gun was they boss. *Rock With Me* was all I could think about, me and my baby playing. I almost wanted one of them to run up on me, but they just standing still, with Reilly's body over to the side, except for one short cat who stepped forward. He was dressed in jeans, t-shirt and a brown leather. Had a big-ass hat on his head, almost like a cowboy hat, but I supposed it was a pimp-brim kinda thing.

"That's our car, man," he said, pointing at Reilly's car.

"You tell 'em, Mongo," a voice behind him shouted.

"Hell, yeah!" another yelled. "White man said he was walking home 'cause somebody took his ride, and that's why he was walking over here. Said he didn't want no trouble."

"We told him it ain't safe, told him to get his honky ass back over to white-ville," another shouted.

"Yeah, and then we commenced to beat his ass," the one in front said, grinning like a cat. "We bet you the one stole his car, now why you over here bothering us," he said.

"Yeah, Mongo, tell his ass he better take that stolen car and get, 'fore we give him some of this here," and the speaker stomped Reilly again. Reilly was fetal, on the ground, a white lump of blackness, dirty and soiled from kicks and hits. I said nothing, but inside I was pleading, "Stop, please stop."

"That's our car now, punk-ass thief," the one named Mongo said again, all big and bad, pointing across the street at Reilly's car. Most of the crowd of watchers had left, scattered when I shot that gun. So it was just me, these young cats, intent on revenge, and Reilly. I wondered if anyone had gone to call the cops, but I couldn't be sure and I didn't want that anyway. I would be locked up too.

"That there our car, now," another dude, stepping up next to Mongo said. "And we gone take it. Come on, y'all," he, said, waving for his boys to follow.

I shot at his feet, making him jump. "Don't try me," I said. "Y'all leave. He ain't bothering y'all. Y'all get the hell outa here right now. Leave him be."

"Aw, man, we just getting back at whitey. Maybe this Motha the .22-Caliber," Mongo shouted. The kid next to him, the Stomper, laughed, and kicked at Reilly again.

"Naw, maybe I am," I shouted, and shot the Stomper in the leg. He cursed, falling on the ground. "Damn, he ain't playin'" one of 'em said, and they began to back up more. This told me none of them was packing, because if they were, I would've been toast. This told me they was probably just a gang of young kids looking for something to do, and stomping a white dude was it tonight. Looking at their faces, I could tell they wasn't that old, maybe the oldest was 15, 16, 17, tops. Anyway, right now, it was punk or be punked. It was my life, and Reilly's too, 'cause them baby-faced mugs could kill, would kill.

"Y'all move. Y'all get going. He ain't nothing but a hippie white dude. Y'all done beat his ass enough," I said, grinning like I was down for them beating an innocent, defenseless cat. But Mongo didn't move, like he was daring me to shoot again, but I knew I had to save my bullets, just in case, because if all them jumped me, I was gone, Reilly too.

"Next one gone be lot higher," I shouted. "I served in 'Nam and I ain't afraid to kill somebody," I lied. I had been in the service, but after 'Nam, and I had only shot in war games and marksmanship. Mongo stared at me, like he wanted to take me one-on-one, then he took a step back, like I had more guns backing me up, or something.

"Thank you, Lord," I whispered.

"We gone get your ass, man. Don't you ever come over here again, Pops," Mongo said, backing up. "We gone let your ass slide, 'cause it's cold and rainy and the cops gone get your sorry ole ass, anyway, with that stolen car."

"Yeah, Mongo," one of his boys said.

"And then we gone get you, too," Mongo said, walking away.

I said nothing back, just stared at 'em, holding my gun out, pointed at Mongo and 'nem, watching as they pimp-walked out of sight, halfway looking back, cussing and threatening. I watched 'til they was gone. Then, I walked over to Reilly, slowly, like they might pounce once they saw me bend down to help. Reilly was hurt real bad. I wasn't no doctor, but I knew he might probably be bleeding internally.

Chapter Six

Timeline:

Thursday, October 2, 1980
A young black man, "E—F—" stops a white pedestrian by driving his car onto the sidewalk, saying that he is an FBI agent. "E—F—" tells the man that he fits the description of the .22-Caliber killer. The man, however, is an off-duty police officer who has just finished his tour. About the same time, a police patrol car is looking for a purse snatcher. The officers recognize his car from the description provided by the white woman whose purse he'd snatched, and arrest him. On the way to the station, "E—F—" kicks out the rear window of the police car and bolts, but is soon recaptured.

Friday, October 3, 1980
Manhunt On in Six States for Sniper Attacking Blacks is the headline for an article in today's edition of the News. And, there are ads about the coming of Ashford and Simpson to Shea's Buffalo and Roberta Flack to Kleinhans Music Hall, as though it's business-as-usual in the community.

Saturday, October 4, 1980
The reward continues to grow. However there is still a wage-related slowdown by the city's police officers. The black community really wonders if a similar slowdown would be tolerated so long if the victims were white. Futhermore, the .22-caliber killings revive the call for a major crimes unit in Western New York.

Sunday, October 5, 1980
The Bills are 5-0, following a comeback win over the San Diego Chargers. But no one cares as much. It's a good season by a bad team, wasted.

Monday, October 6, 1980
The desperation of the investigation becomes apparent when Buffalo Homicide Chief Leo L. Donovan meets for five hours with an astrologer and a psychic in hopes of finding the killer. The chief suggests that a psychic and an astrologer *have given us some interesting information that is being checked out.* Donovan's desperation, and that of the whole force is

clear from this comment: *I don't see any harm in it. When you don't have anything going for you, any input can be a help.*

Tuesday, October 7, 1980

A number of law enforcement officials, including Chief Donovan, speak with local black leaders at a BUILD meeting. After the meeting, BUILD announces the forming of a people's commission with two main aims: an end to the police slowdown and the assignment of black officers to cases involving violence against blacks. BUILD also announces that it is reviving its Deacons for Defense self-protection committee and that the group is going to help blacks apply to carry pistols. Blacks also begin riding shotgun in cabs to protect drivers in the community. Blacks suspect a conspiracy and charge genocide. But Police Commissioner Cunningham maintains that he sees no signs of a plot to harm blacks.

Johnny's Story, continued:

I picked Reilly up off the muddy ground and carried him to the car, kinda sliding him, dragging him, 'cause he was dead weight. "I'm sorry, man. I'm sorry. It's my fault," was all I could whisper, as I drug him, walking backwards toward the car, so I could see if they returned. He was beat bad, man, blood all over his face and clothes. He tried to speak but couldn't. Dude's eyes were beat shut. Now, I knew Laney'd never forgive me, and never, ever come home. She'd think I did it to him to get back at her. Days before she'd left, I'd said,

"I hate white people."

"All white people didn't enslave or hurt us, John. So why the blanket indictment of all whites? That's stupid."

"Then I'm stupid."

She didn't respond, just gave me the stare. No, she'd never come back now. This dude was her favorite teacher. She'd think I hurt him on purpose. As I carried him, all his dirt and mud was getting on me. He was heavy and it was taking too long. What if they did come back? I'd have to shoot to kill. Or I could drop his ass, throw his keys next to his body, and walk on home. No, that would be killing him for sure, even if they didn't come back. This was no place for a white man. I knew what Laney would have wanted me to do.

When I accused her of liking her teacher, she said, "No, hon, I like his mind. He encourages me to think, all of his students to think and to expand their mental territories."

"You sure this all that white man trying to expand with you?"

"Johnny, you're just plain ignorant," she said, turning away. Maybe I was ignorant. But I wasn't no damn killer.

When I got him to the car, I pinned him up against it with one arm and opened the door with the other. "I'ma drive you to the hospital," I said, not knowing if he understood. What if this white man died? Here I was, driving his car and carrying a gun. And he's all beat up? If he didn't make it, sure was gonna look like I did it, and who was gone testify that I didn't? Not even Laney. "Lord, help me," I prayed.

He groaned, making some kinda sound.

I kept praying, saying, "Thank you, Jesus" and "Yes, Lord" like in Laney's church. I stuffed him in the seat and buckled him in tight, like he was Baby Girl. "Please, Lord," I prayed. Maybe this white man was dying, in the middle of a crazy city with a race war waging. "Please, Lord, please, don't let him die," was all I could think, all I could pray. A dead white man in a car that belonged to him, and I'm driving. Prison time; probably never see my family again. "Don't die, please don't die," I whispered in his ear, almost kissing it.

Driving, I had the radio turned down low, to listen to the news, hear if there was anything about him or news on the killer. Where was I gonna take him? The hospital or police station would ask too many questions, and I'd be caught. That would be like turning myself in to the cops. After driving in circles, around Fillmore and Ferry, around Humbolt Park, I knew: Deliverance Church. They said the pastor of Laney's church, Rev. Williamson, had a gift of healing, and on a Saturday, he just might be there, getting ready for service tomorrow. I turned the radio to a gospel station, and headed toward Deliverance.

Timeline:

October 8, 1980

A black taxi driver, Parler Edwards, age 71, of 208 Grape Street, is found in the trunk of his car in Amherst, a suburb of the city. His head was bashed in with a lead pipe, and his heart was cut out and taken.

October 9, 1980

Another taxi driver, Ernest Jones, age 40, is found dead beside the Niagara River in Tonawanda, a suburb. Like with Edwards, his heart was cut out, and his body was dragged some 60-feet along blacktop.

Police Chief Donovan maintains that the two recent murders of black men are not related to the earlier four slayings. "There is no evidence in any way to connect them."

The News prints a story, *Killer In Mutilation Is Bigot, UB Prof Theorizes*. According to this professor, *It seems like blacks are being sought out by the murderers*. The black community wonders why the hell a white professor is needed for this conclusion, when we knew it all along.

There is a cross-burning on Brunswick Avenue, in the heart of the community. Police attribute it to blacks attempting to incite racial unrest, as though there isn't already unrest. Six young black men stand on a corner across from police officers putting out the burning cross.

They shout, *Let it burn* and *Call the TV stations*. A black man pulls up in a car and takes photos of the officers with the cross. Some believe that blacks erected the cross.

A direct telephone hot line to the investigation is finally set up. The Police Benevolent Association puts up money, adding to the amount of the total reward.

City Councilman Arthur O. Eve and Rev. Charles H. Fisher, III, local black leaders, call for calm, saying, *No one should travel unless they travel with someone else*.

And New York State Governor Hugh Carey orders the State Police to join in the search for the .22-Caliber Killer. The black community feels that this, too, is long overdue.

Johnny's story, continued:

I left him in the car, taking my lunch pail with me. The church door was unlocked, so I walked on in. The sanctuary was small, seating maybe 200 people, 300 tops. It had dark brown pews, red carpet and white walls with Bible verses and pictures on them.

"I need healing," I said, standing at the back of the church, looking at a small group of people up front, some women and a little boy. They were all around the altar, on their knees, cleaning, or something. "I need healing," I repeated, louder this time.

Only the little boy rose up, turning around and looking at me. I stared at him, and he stared back. His big eyes reminded of Nisey, when she got scared or was telling a lie. He was a skinny little kid, dressed in blue jeans and a Buffalo Sabres sweatshirt who reminded me of myself at that age, but he didn't say nothing, just tapped one of the women, and then she turned around too. One by one, the women, who'd been kneeling down, praying or cleaning the carpet, I couldn't tell, rose and faced me. They were all dressed in cleaning clothes, head rags and aprons. I recognized a couple of them, but didn't know their names.

"I need healing, y'all," I repeated. Then I just stood there waiting, funky and dirty, hoping, praying. These women and the boy must have been

working on the altar and the pews, cleaning them up, because I noticed cleaning rags and a bucket on the floor near the front pew. The women were all dressed alike, in long dresses or skirts and big, loose blouses. They reminded me of Miss Florence Shellman, who used to baby sit us kids. But Miss Florence was a snuff dipper, and these ladies called that *sin*.

"Who are you? And what do you want?" one of the women asked, shaking her cleaning rags at me.

"We don't have no money," another said, her hands on her hips.

"Healing," I said, and began walking up to that altar, toward them. I was holding my pail tight, cradling it like I used to do Nisey, when she was a baby. "Just healing and prayer," I said walking closer, but not wanting to scare 'em, 'cause they was all I had. If I couldn't come here, where could I go? "I just come here for help, not harm," I said, clutching my pail.

Then, one of them stepped forward. "Hello, Brother John Smith," she said, speaking softly, but firmly, like we was in a business meeting. She smiled, like she knew me, and then I recalled her name, Mother Della Black. "We haven't seen you in awhile," she said. She was over the church choir 'Laney and them sung in. Choir could jam; used to rock the church with songs like *Sweeping Through the City* and *Climbing up the Mountain*.

"It's Sister Delaney's husband, Brother Smith," she said to the others.

"Praise the Lord," and "Glory, Jesus," some of the women said.

"Yes, Lord, Sister Delaney said you were coming back to the Lord, and now you're here," another one, Mother Lula Mae Cherry, I think was her name, said. She smiled, brown and warm, like I was her son, coming to be baptized.

"I need y'all to pray for somebody. He's in the car."

"Well, go tell him to come on in."

"I can't. He can't walk. He's hurt."

"Then why didn't you take him to the hospital?"

"This here is a hospital, Lula," Mother Black said.

"For souls, Della, for souls."

"But don't Pastor always talk about how God can heal?"

"I need some help to bring him in," I said, turning toward the door.

"Manny! Go and help Brother John Smith," the third lady said. Then I remembered her name; she was Mother Williamson, the Reverend's wife. Delaney said she had a "gift" of tongues and prayer.

"Help him do what?" the lanky kid asked. He looked to be maybe nine-years-old, ten, tops. He was supposed to have been wiping a pew, but was really just standing around, gawking.

"Help him do whatever he needs, boy."

The boy walked with me to the car. He walked behind me, like he was scared. I thought of the boys who had beat up Reilly. This boy wasn't really that different from them, just probably had a tough, praying Granny.

"Oh, God," he said as I opened the door. "You do this to him? Why you beat up this white man like that?"

"I ain't do it," I said, as I pulled on Reilly's body to pick him up, off the seat.

As the boy and I brought him in, I knew it looked a sight and, I don't know why, I looked down at the clean carpet and my muddy shoes. But I couldn't apologize no more.

"Jesus help me. What happened here?" Mother Black and one of the women looked at him like he was dead already.

"Is he dead, boy? I mean, Brother Smith? What did you do to him? What happened, what in heaven's name happened?"

"Here, set him down on this here bench," Mother Williamson said, pointing to the front pew.

".22-Caliber," I said, as we carried him toward the front.

"You bringing that there killer in here? Looks like he got what was coming to him. Eye for eye," Mother Cherry said.

"No, he's not the .22-Caliber. But they thought he was, or at least said he was. Group of kids."

"Black kids?" Mother Black asked.

"Who else?" Mother Cherry said, shaking her head.

"And Brother Smith, why are you all up in this?" Mother Williamson said, staring at me as though this was the killer. But her face said, "I can see why your wife left you." And I knew that they knew.

"He was Delaney's teacher, and I hitched a ride with him."

"So, how did he get beaten up like this?" Mother Cherry was dabbing his forehead and praying in whispers. "You sure you didn't do this to him, son?"

Chapter Seven

Timeline:

October 10, 1980
Police See Peril of Vigilantism is one headline in the local paper.

The police warn whites to stay away from black neighborhoods, "until this killer is caught."

Columnist Ray Hall writes an impassioned *Open Letter* to the killer: *For Heaven's Sake, Give Yourself Up.* Hall continues, *Your legacy is a burning cross.*

A black auto worker comes forward to report that a club-wielding white man in a van threatened his life, saying, *I'll kill you nigger.*

Black leaders question the police about a metal projectile that hits a bus carrying a black church choir from Buffalo to Syracuse. According to one Rev., *It could well be a bullet.*

Blacks strike back, pelting cars of white passengers with rocks, bottles, bricks and sticks on Jefferson Street and Sycamore Street and elsewhere throughout the community.

Other blacks, claiming to be narcotics detectives stop a white couple on St. Louis Street and fire shots at their car.

Today, Rev. Jesse Jackson is in town at the urging of BUILD. Jackson joins local officials for a televised meeting about the killings. Later, he preaches in BUILD Town Hall, urging the crowd to avoid revenge and violence, and 600 black voices respond to his call with the chant, *I Am Somebody. I Am Somebody.* The evening ends with the singing of *We Shall Overcome*, yet prior to his talk, the BUILD switchboard receives an assassination threat against Jackson's life: *Jesse Jackson will be shot*, a male voice says, and then utters racial slurs before hanging up.

Tonight, Ashford and Simpson and Larry Graham play at Shea's Buffalo Theatre, while Roberta Flack plays Kleinhan's Music Hall, like Buffalo is a Mecca of black culture, rather than a citadel of insanity and black death.

Johnny's Story, continued:

For a moment, we all stared at Reilly, slumped over the pew like a drunk. He smelled like blood and filthy sidewalks. His eyes were busted shut. His mouth was bloody and his shirt was torn to tatters. They'd kicked holes in his clothes, stomped their mud on him, and one of them had hit him repeatedly with a baseball bat. His ribs might be broken. I

hoped I'd gotten to him in time. Looking at him, I knew they wondered why I hadn't taken him to the hospital. I wondered if they'd figured out that I couldn't even have dropped him off there, leaving his car and his battered body for someone to find. Same reason I couldn't take him inside a hospital: the cops.

"Yes, Lord Jesus, Yes, Lord," Sister Cherry hummed while stroking his forehead with a rag, probably one of those blessed oil cloths Laney placed on Nisey when Baby Girl wasn't feeling good. "Yes, Lord Jesus, Yeah, Lord," she hummed, touching his face and shoulders like this white man was her son, her child.

Mother Black stared at me. "Didn't his wife, Sister Delaney, say something about . . . "

"Not now, Lula, hush," Mother Williamson said. "We just need to pray," she said, "We just need to pray," and she reached out her arms, her hands, for someone to take them, so we could gather around him. I took her outstretched hand and I grabbed the boy's, who was standing next to me.

Taking my hand, the boy spoke, "If he's the .22-Caliber Killer, let him die. Let's don't waste no prayers on that honkie man!"

"Boy, keep quiet. Did Jesus let you die?"

"People still die. Some white man killing black people, 'pecially boys and men."

"But you don't have to die in your sins, knucklehead boy. And we ain't gonna let this man suffer without praying for his body and soul," Mother Black said, cuffing the boy upside his head.

"Ouch, that hurt!" The boy flinched from the hit.

"Supposed to hurt, now shut up, before I put a real hurting on your insolent behind, Manny."

Mother Williamson released her hands from mine. "Lay him down on the altar, y'all," she ordered Manny and me.

We laid Reilly's body down on the crimson carpet. One of the women, Sister Cherry, put a purple seat cushion beneath his head. Another covered him partially with a light, white, shawl. Cherry and Black started to sing, "Yes, Lord. Yessss, Lord. Yessss Lord. Yessss, Lord. Yeahhhh, Lord. Yeahhh, Lord." He was in a fetal position, like a baby in the womb.

They intoned "yes Lord," so loud it sounded like the church was full. They sang, "Yes, Lord," like God was in the midst, or coming soon; I closed my eyes as the singing gave way to prayers. Next thing, they were touching my forehead, wiping it with that oil, and I knew they were anointing his head with oil, too.

"Oh, Lord, we bless your holy name. We magnify your name. We exalt your name. We humbly ask you to save and heal this man, our brother.

Though he's white and there's a white on the loose killing our people, we understand you're a God of mercy. Whether he's that killer or just an innocent victim of hate, we ask you to save him, Lord. Save his soul. Spare his life, heal him Lord. We know, oh Lord, that no one is innocent, that all have sinned and come short. But we also know that by your stripes we are healed. Heal him Lord. Save him and make him whole . . ."

With my eyes closed, I didn't know which church mother was speaking or if they all were; it sounded like a whisper and a song. It sounded like Reilly was moaning and praying, too. I couldn't open my eyes. I was afraid God's magic wouldn't work if I did. Afraid Reilly might be dead if I jinxed it by watching. Next thing, I was lying on the floor beside him. Our bodies warm, close, I thought of Middle Passage, slave ships. Were white people ever in the hold, as prisoners?

Wouldn't that be punishment, to put a white in the hold with a bunch of African *niggers*? Well, these *nigger* women were praying for Reilly's body and soul, as they were praying for mine. Eventually . . . they began to clap and praise God and pray-sing. "Oh, Lord. Thank you, Lord. Thank you, Jesus!"

Somebody was beating a tambourine and somebody was praying in tongues. "Thank you, Jesus! Thank you Lord!" I wondered if the shouting signified Reilly's deliverance from death, or from life? Would they shout for glory if this white man died? Maybe they would if his soul was saved, but I needed him to live.

"Yeah, Lord. Yeah, Lord." I recognized Mother Williamson's voice, praying and speaking in unknown tongues. Tongues surrounded me. Hands anointed my forehead, torso, my limbs, touching me, slapping me in Jesus' name.

"Thank you, Lord." I began to pray-sing too, lying there on that carpet, "Thank you for my wife and daughter and for Bill Reilly."

Maybe I had wanted him to die. That's why I took his car. I had wanted to hurt him, to destroy a white man. That's why I didn't have the guts to take him to the hospital. But as the praying, the tongues, the tambourines, the clapping engulfed us, Bill Reilly's body and mine so close, I touched his shoulder and arm and prayed, too.

Eventually, the prayers and singing stopped. Eventually, I opened my eyes and rose to my knees.

"You've been saved, Brother John Smith," little Manny said, smiling, reaching out his hand to me.

"I have, huh?" Bill wasn't beside me on the floor. When I turned toward the pews, he was sitting on the front row. He looked better, as though he might make it.

"You spoke in tongues, Brother Johnny," Manny said, still pumping my hand, smiling, "that means you've been saved. I've been tarrying for months and I ain't spoken in tongues yet."

"Manny, hush, boy," Mother Black said, popping the boy upside his head again. "That's because you're so bad, Manny. I got a new name for you, 'Mischievous Manny'." The boy frowned, but said nothing.

"How is he?" I asked, rising, nodding at Reilly, who seemed to be resting, sleeping on the pew.

"He's better for sure," Mother Brownlee said.

"He's healed," Manny said.

"Thank you," I said.

"Sit down, next to your friend," Mother Williamson said, motioning to the pew. "We ain't done with y'all." Sister Cherry was holding a tray with communion wafers and shot glasses of grape juice.

"This is His body, broken for you," Mother Black said, as Sister Cherry handed me a wafer. I took one and ate it. Cherry stuffed a wafer in Reilly's mouth.

"This is His blood, shed for the remission of your sins," Mother Black said, and I responded by taking one of the tiny cups and drinking from it. Cherry held the tiny cup to Reilly's lips and some of it went in, while the rest trickled down the side of his face, like a trail of blood. After the Communion, they sang one more song, *I Know It Was the Blood*. They sang verse after verse, clapping, looking at us, or shutting their eyes and sing-praying, *His blood came streaming down* and *One day when I was lost, He died upon the Cross. I know it was the blood for me.*

Eventually, they stopped; I looked at Reilly, sleeping again, slumped over on the pew, and then I looked at them. A rag-tag bunch of old black women. None of 'em probably had degrees or big credentials. The biggest title they probably ever had was *Church Mother, Deaconess*, or *Momma*, but they had saved us, this educated white man with a Ph.D., and me. I wondered if he would ever know. If any of them, rich, smart white people, would ever know, the dignity and power of these old black women. They reminded me of Momma. I rose up.

"We're better," I said. "Better," and I hoped they got my meaning. "Can Manny help me get him to the car?"

"I'll help you," Mother Black said.

As we were walking him back down the aisle, she asked, "Where did you get a car, Brother Johnny? Your wife didn't mention that y'all had gotten one."

"His car," I said. "I'm driving him."

"So you really are a good Samaritan," she said.

Reilly mumbled something, and I hoped she couldn't understand his words. I didn't know if they would call the cops, but I figured they would call Laney.

Once he was buckled securely in the car, Black looked me in the eye and squeezed my shoulder. "I don't care what you've done. Take him to a hospital, to get him some help, you hear me?"

"Yes, ma'am."

"Prayer works, son," she continued, touching my shoulder, squeezing it. "Now make sure you don't just come by the church when you're in desperation."

"Yes, Ma'am."

"And maybe if you do, then the Lord will mend your marriage." Her eyes pierced me like her words, and I didn't need to ask if she knew where my family was. She did, but wasn't about to tell me. She did, and Laney was going to hear all about this.

"I'm gonna take him to the hospital," I said, touching her hand, thinking of my deceased mom. "I'm going to get him more help." Then, I let go of her and started the car. Driving off, I waved one last time.

Maybe those kids hadn't almost killed him, or maybe those prayers worked. All I knew was that it hadn't been as hard getting Reilly in his car this time, and he looked different.

As I drove I remembered when I'd attended church and watched Delaney in that choir. This was her family's church; she'd grown up in it. She was their daughter, but I wasn't their son. Elder Williamson wouldn't marry us, because he didn't believe in marrying Saved and Unsaved. So we'd married at the Falls in a little rinky, dinky, wedding chapel. Our reception was a dinner for two at a restaurant watching the water cascade over the cliffs. When I attended church with Laney, I got to know 'em, her old church friends: Daryl and Gary and Lorenzo and Sheral and Ruby and Christine and Willie. Some of them, like Andrew, who locked himself in the church one Friday and by Sunday, he could play the organ like nobody's business. Or Sister Dockery, who came to church one Friday night on crutches, but walked out of the place. Now I knew a little bit better why Laney sometimes cried when she talked about this church, these people. I knew better why her eyes sparkled and she looked like she was seeing God, when they sang, *Climbing Up the Mountain, tryin' to reach the top*. Now, I knew better . . . but what I was gone to do with it, this knowledge?

"Home." Bill Reilly said something; he was kinda slumped over, but was looking at me out the corner of an eye.

"What?" I looked at him, then back at road. The sky was still dreary, like it was gonna storm.

"Home," he said again, louder, almost like an order, like he was taking charge.

"Hospital," I said, 'cause I wanted him to know I cared and was gone do the right thing.

"Home, please," he kinda muttered. "My fiancé is a doc."

"Where is home?" I asked, like he might trick me, when I had tricked him. I didn't trust him, but maybe we had to trust each other.

"Drive me home," he said, softly, pointing at the windshield, showing he'd direct my way.

Chapter Eight

Barbershop talk—

"Gets to a point," Johnny said, "when the people who know your story, they're dead, or out of touch, so it's even more important, like you're carrying their stories within yours. Maybe that's all you got left, memories and stories. That's how I feel, y'all, like dead friends' stories done walked into mine, so mine is bigger now, expanded. And the weight is heavier."

"He ain't heavy, he's my bruh?" Kwame laughed.

"Yeah, I guess so," Johnny said.

That night, I looked at my notes and thought about burning them. Why was I doing this? To gain tenure? To gain the favor of some white people, to have them tell me that my work was good? Didn't I despise them, too?

My cell phone buzzed: Bridgette's number. I considered not answering, since we basically said nothing new each time we talked:

"How was work?"

"Work was work."

"How's A.B.?"

"He's okay."

"Tell everybody I said 'hi.'"

"I will."

Our phone conversations usually ended in less than ten minutes, so what the hell? I could make them longer, by feigning interest, but we still wouldn't say much. I picked up on the fourth ring.

"Hello, Doc."

"Hey, A.B."

"How'd you know it was me?"

"I know your voice, man."

"You know why I'm calling?"

"You want some money? To buy a video game or something? And no, you can't drive the Lex," I said, referring to the car I'd left his mom to drive.

"Naw, man. Called to see when you comin' home. Mom misses you."

"I miss her, too," I lied. I didn't miss anyone, anymore.

"Doc, if you don't come back soon, don't ever come back, man."

"What . . . ?"

"You deserted us, man, and I'm getting to hate you, like I do my white-ass daddy." He paused, as though to let his words sink in. "I hate this white blood in me, man. If I could cut myself and drain it all out, I would, man."

"You're not thinking of doing anything crazy, are you, A.B.?"

"Call me Black, man! Call me Black!"

"Okay, whatever, just so I know you don't do anything crazy."

"What the hell do it matter to you? You up there, and my mom, she needs you, or she used to, but we used to you being gone now, man, so don't come back, just don't come back . . . I know you're working on a book and shit, and I know you send mom money and pay for the house and all, but damn, man, you deserted us. My mom, I caught her crying after the last time y'all talked, like you said something to hurt her, and I don't play that shit, man. Not with my mom. So maybe you best just stay away for good, man..."

I thought I heard him begin to sob, so I said, "Maybe we both ought to hang up, A.B. Maybe . . ."

"Maybe you can't call me A.B. no more, neither. Call me Anderson or Black, and like I said, don't be coming back at all, unless you back to stay. Make up your f'ing mind, man! I'm tired a this shit!"

"You threatening me, 'Anderson,' or 'Black,' or whatever the hell you want me to call you?"

"Just know I'ma hurt you if you keep hurtin' momma. That's all I got ta say. I'll get your ass good!" He hung up, and I listened to the silence.

I listened to what I should have said: "A.B., I hate white blood, too." "A.B., you're a hybrid, and hybridity is in now. You just gotta know how to use it." "A.B., no, I am not coming back, not to that. You're young and you don't understand."

But did I? Did I understand?

Timeline:

Friday, October 10, 1980

Headline: *Attempted Strangling Of a Black Man Foiled by a Nurse at Medical Center.* According to the news article, *A man matching the description of the .22-Caliber Killer attacked a black male detox patient, Colvin Cole, in the Erie County Medical Center today after telling the patient, "I hate niggers." Cole was on the seventh floor of the hospital. Erie County D.A. Cosgrove says the attacker tried to strangle the man with a cord. However,*

when a nurse opened the room to Cole's room, the attacker, leaning over the bed, mumbled, "He's fallen and hurt himself," and then fled.

Johnny's Story, continued:

Pulling in his driveway, I turned out the light, turned off the engine and rolled on up. It was a big, Tudor style house, with a nice-sized front lawn. I bet it had a nice backyard, the kind I wanted one day for Nisey to play in. I closed the car doors softly, quietly, because what I wanted to do was get him in there, and get out, with nobody knowing. Open the door, shove him in, and split. I had a mind to leave him on the front step but this was Buffalo, NY in October, and it could get down to around freezing at night. It had started to snow.

"Almost there," I said, holding him as I struggled to walk with him, into his house. I used his keys to open their front door. Once in, there was a little entryway and flights of stairs, both up and down.

"Bill! Bill! Oh, Bill!"

A white woman screaming, standing at the top of the stairs. My arm was around him, holding him up, the weight of his body on me. "Bill! Bill! Bill!" she was screaming.

"Get off of him, leave him alone. Get out! Get out!" she was screaming, running down the stairs at us, while I was just going to deposit him right there and leave. She rammed us with her body, and started pushing me, trying to scrape me off of him while grabbing for him, but he was clutching onto me, so I couldn't get loose. He was between the two of us, on the first two steps going up. She had hold of him, too, from the steps above, but I couldn't let him go, because we'd both fall back outside, or down the other flight of stairs, leading to a lower level.

"Get out," she screamed, "Let go! Get out!"

"Just gonna help him up, lady," I said. As she tugged on him, I pushed, clutching him while he held onto me. I thought of tug-of-war in grade school, and Bill was the rope between us. Neither let go. She was pulling on him, while I was holding on so he wouldn't tumble back. Eventually, either through her pulling or his climbing, we made it to the top of the stairs, and she began moving toward a sofa. He dropped down.

"Now, get out!" She screamed with a look which said, *Nigger, why'd you do this?*

"Okay."

"Oh Bill, oh Bill, what happened?" She was touching him, patting him like a baby, talking fast. She knelt in front of him, between her man's legs. "Oh Bill, what happened? What did he do to you? How did

this happen? Oh Bill. I'm calling the police," she said, looking at me. "So you better go, now."

I threw his keys on the sofa, beside him. No way I could take that car now. I'd have to find them on foot.

"I'm out," I said, turning to leave, when she reached up, grabbing my arm. She was a little white lady, maybe no more than a hundred pounds and change, but I couldn't resist her. If I did, she might say I hurt her, wrestled her, touched her the wrong way. "I just wanna leave, lady."

She moved in front of me, to block my way. She was a white picket fence, which said, "you're not going anywhere."

"Saved me," he mumbled. "Kids and car."

"What, Billy?" she looked over at the couch, to him. "Just hold on, dear. I'll be right there. Now, you," she said. "What do you have to say for yourself . . ."

"Let him go," Bill said, a little louder. "Saved me."

"He's healed," I said, not moving, staring back at her. But her face said, "I hate you, nigger, and I'm going to stop you."

I looked away from her, around the room, and saw things I could take and use for money to get home. It wasn't a fancy place, but its furnishings said, *class*. Nice old woodwork, and brass metal knobs and fixtures. Fall colors, rich, inviting autumn tones, gold and burnt oranges. But I wasn't invited. I could imagine, on another day, at another time, shooting the bull with Bill, an invited guest, but right now, I was an intruder. She was blocking me. I had no money, and it was a long walk back. I'd have to push her out the way and get to stepping.

In her hand was a fireplace poker. "Bill, I don't understand what's happened. And he can't leave, this, this, thug; he can't leave until I say so. I'm calling the police, Billy." I didn't know where she got it from or grabbed it. Maybe she'd had it all the time or had reached for it under a chair. I didn't know. All I knew was, I could easily take it from her, snatch her frail white behind like I was the black rapist criminal she assumed, and toss her on the couch, next to him. So I could leave.

"You better move," I said, at her. "I don't want trouble." She was 5'2", 5'3", tops, dressed in jeans and a UB t-shirt. I could pick her up and toss her aside.

"Not until I get some answers," she said. "My cousin's on the force," she added. "So I want some answers."

"He's got 'em," I said, nodding at Bill. "I just want to get to my family," I said, trying to emphasize to this white woman that I didn't want her, didn't want to hurt them. She lifted that poker like she was gone use it, stepped back, like she was gonna thrust me through with that stick. She swung, and I jumped out the way, toward Bill and the sofa.

"Let him go," Bill said, as loud as he probably could. "What are you doing, Amber? Let him go!" His body leaned forward like he would get up if he could. His face was a map of tears, soil, and blessed oil. "Please. I'll explain. Please." She looked at him, and then at me.

I wanted to close my eyes. I needed Laney. Nisey. I needed Mother Black from the church. *A lone black man is a danger in this society*, the brothas on the street had taught me, *angry, anxious, and aware* of how whites saw me. How this white woman saw me. Facing a white woman, no way I'd win.

"Please," I said, repeating Bill, but looking at her.

"Whoever you are, I don't know why you brought him home after doing this to him, so now you've gotten revenge on an innocent white guy. This entire damned city's gone crazy. So now you've gotten revenge on my Billy. You, you, you better leave fast, before I call the police," she said, but she didn't drop that poker, and she was still blocking my way. I didn't want to have to hurt her, but I would.

"Saved my life from a gang of kids."

"They thought he was the .22-Caliber," I said.

Her white face was hard; her jaws were sharp. Her eyes were like pins and needles that I could feel pricking me, sticking into me. "Why did you blacks do this? Don't you people realize that most of us don't want to harm you? Can't you fathom that all whites are not racist?"

"I just want to go."

"My Billy's innocent," she said. "You can't just take revenge indiscriminately." She still hadn't moved, but now she was staring at her man.

Then, Bill spoke a little louder, "Amber, before you let him go, would you go get my '77/78 class folders? There's something I want to give to John."

She looked at him with eyes that said *no*.

"Please, Amber," he whispered, gesturing with one hand, and she moved.

"John," he said to me, and I turned toward him, looking down at him slumped on the sofa, obviously still in pain, "don't forget your lunch pail. It's in the center console." His eyes were kinda closed, like he didn't want to look at me, or maybe he was just saving strength.

"Delaney Smith," he said, when she returned with some folders. "His wife," he said, and she stared at me. "Give him her papers."

She dropped the folder at his feet, as though surprised or maybe to avoid contact with me. I walked over, knelt down and went through it 'til I found Laney's papers in a plastic binder. I took 'em out.

"Thanks," I said, touching one of his hands, which rested on the couch.

She stepped aside and let me pass, but that poker was still in her right hand, and I was afraid she was gone stab me with it in the back or hurl it, so I jumped down the stairs.

In the car, I got my lunch pail with my gun in it and in the console I found money. Tens, twenties; I took thirty, enough to get a cab to the city. Enough to help me find my family. I felt her eyes on me from the front window, but I didn't care. Opening the lunch pail, I folded up Laney's papers and stuffed them beside my gun. I stuffed the money in my pockets. Then, I locked the car door.

Timeline:

October 11, 1980
In desperation, Buffalo police visit Son of Sam Killer David Berkowitz in Attica State Prison, hoping to gain insight from the crazed killer. The police also scour the city for self-proclaimed Klansmen and Nazis.

Black cabbies are full of fear, since Edwards and Jones were killed while making their rounds, trying to find early morning fares. *But I have to make a living,* one black cabbie says. Like with the cabbies, Blacks throughout the city arm themselves, not expecting the police to defend them. Black men ride shotgun in cabs driven by other blacks.

Police in the Genesee and Fillmore stations report a series of attacks in which cars carrying whites were fired upon or pelted with rocks. *Police See Peril Of Vigilantism On East Side,* one news headline reads. Mayor Griffin reminds citizens that Buffalo is *the city of good neighbors.*

Officers Jones and Owens, two black officers, form a task force to help keep peace in the black community. *Some innocent white people are going to get hurt,* says Jones.

More blacks carry guns on the street, and there are multiple reported attacks on whites:

Four black men attack a white man walking down Peckham Street.

Two black men walk up on a white man's parked car while he sits with his girlfriend. One of the men is carrying a gun and the other a billy club.

According to the police, *There are a lot of crazy people, both black and white, who will use this situation to their advantage.*

Republican V.P. candidate George Bush visits Buffalo and tells reporters that Ronald Reagan, for whom he is in Buffalo campaigning for the presidency, is a foe of racism and bias. This is in opposition to Rev.

64

Jesse Jackson's remarks a day earlier concerning Reagan's use of racially-coded phrases such as *state's rights*. Bush also praises Buffalo for *keeping calm* amidst the racial tension created by the murders. But he is wrong, dead wrong: our city isn't calm. It's in chaos.

Johnny's Story, continued:

As I walked away, up French Road toward Niagara Falls Boulevard, I didn't think about how long it was going to take to get home. I just wanted to get out of white folks' land.

As I walked on the Boulevard, I held my thumb up, to hitch a ride, or catch a cab but after three white cabbies drove by, I knew I was invisible. I was humming a church song, *Burden Down, Lord, Burden Down, since I laid my burden down.* I wanted to get home, to my home, just to hunker down and wait. Wait for what? I really didn't know. Maybe for the white man to get me or my wife to come back, or Jesus to return. I didn't care. Couldn't even hitch a ride, but with each step, I was closer. Really, I knew I shouldn't take a cab or hitch a ride in a white man's car. Might be the .22-Caliber . . . Death.

I hoped these white folks whizzing by thought I was just another black janitor going back to the city. When I had left Billy Reilly's house, I was walking slow, but now I almost jogging, run-walking to keep warm. The air, coming down from the Canada and the Falls was blowing through me. Then I remembered that the city bus came to the University, UB, out here, so maybe I wasn't going to have to walk so far. But when I turned around to look behind me, no bus in sight.

Then this cop car pulled up on the sidewalk in front of me. Another cop car pulled behind me. I looked to the fields on my side, but I couldn't run. They'd shoot me dead, .22-Caliber chaos or not. I stopped dead in my tracks, even before they said, "Halt, police!"

I dropped my lunch pail, put my hands over my head.

"We got a call about you, Johnny. We're taking you in."

I was behind the cage in that cop car and they had my stuff. One of the cops said something about, "She alleges you assaulted him, stole his car and his money. She said she wasn't going to call us until she found the cash missing."

I wanted to shout out, "But I saved him." I wanted to shout, "They was beating his ass, but I saved him," but I knew better, before I got mine beaten, so instead I tried to rest, take myself someplace else, playing with Nisey, making love to my Laney, or eating dinner with 'em. *Burden Down, Lord, Burden Down.* I sang church songs and thought about sleep.

Chapter Nine

Timeline:

Sunday, October 12, 1980
Another cross is burned in the Buffalo area, this one in nearby Lockport. Four whites were charged with burning a 13' by 6' cross; according to the police, they were drunken.

More blacks needed on the police force, black police officers say. These are the same black officers who set up a security detail for the Rev. Jesse Jackson after the death threats against him.

Erie County D.A. Edward Cosgrove addresses the local chapter of PUSH, to discuss the effort to apprehend the killer, and to try to calm the fears of blacks. Cosgrove also takes to the radio, urging calm, restraint, and patience with the police.

Monday, October 13, 1980
The slayings of six black men here and in neighboring cities are the work *of someone who is deranged* and will be solved if Buffalo residents *keep our cool,* Mayor Griffin says today . . . Meanwhile, Collin Cole, 37, the black man whose larynx was crushed in an attack by the .22-Caliber while he lay in a hospital bed talks to officials investigating the case. ECMC and other area hospitals increase security due to the hospital attack. And U.S. Attorney General Benjamin Civiletti pledges to send an assistant, Drew S. Days, to work on the case.

Meanwhile, community leader William Gaiter, head of the Institute for People Enterprises on Jefferson Avenue, begins distributing black ribbons to be worn on the left shoulder as a sign of mourning. The NAACP and other groups announce the plan of a unity rally to be held this coming Sunday at City Hall.

Throughout the city, among leaders and followers, all agree this call for unity is sorely needed, as blacks continue attacking whites, in retaliation.

Tuesday, October 14, 1980
A white man, "JFC," 23, is shot by a black man when he answers a knock at his front door. "JFC" is hospitalized in fair condition as police work to figure out if the shooting was sparked by the killing spree. But the black community knows. This shooting was the third time in the past week we had fired on whites. It was like James Brown sings in his song: *The Big Payback.* The payback continues in Buffalo, and it is televised.

Johnny's Story, continued:

When we got to the precinct, they charged me with assault and theft. They also charged me with carrying a concealed weapon and no permit. And there wasn't nothing I could say. At one point, I tried to, and said, "But I saved him from a gang of black kids. They was beating him . . ."

"Shut up," one of the cops yelled in my face, looking like he wanted to hit me. "Shut the hell up, liar! Ain't we got enough insanity in this city without nig-"

"Without Negroes taking out vengeance on defenseless whites," one of the other cops interrupted.

"But I ain't do nothing," I said. "He was my wife's teacher."

"That just makes it worse. Looks like he trusted you and you took advantage. Be better for you if you 'fess up. Otherwise, you need to shut up, because you had his car, his keys, money and a gun. His fiancée said you looked like you wanted to do some harm and maybe steal some more when you were in the house, so she had to arm herself with a poker."

"We prayed for him. The Lord healed him . . ."

"Shut up, Johnny. There's too much evidence against you. And no one in that neighborhood corroborates your story about a gang beating a white man."

"Do I get to make a call?"

"Even a good lawyer's not gonna help you, unless you 'fess up, dude."

"I wanna call my home, my wife."

As they showed me where to call from, one of them said, "He's at the hospital now and depending upon the extent of his injuries, this could become worse for you." He grinned.

Standing at that phone, leaning against that grey, cold wall, I prayed. I didn't know where else to call but home. *Burden Down, Burden Down.* These white men wanted to kill me, lock me up. Same as Bill's fiancée, Amber, they thought I'd tried to kill him, hurt him, like a black man couldn't care for a white man in the middle of this racial madness. Laney saw something in him, like he was different. Maybe he was.

Our just phone rang. It was probably dark outside by now. It rang and rang. I didn't know what time it was, but they had clocks in this jail somewhere. I thought about the commercial, *Do you know where your children are?* Momma used to use that to say *time for bed* on weekends. On most school nights we never even heard it.

Our phone rang. "Answer it," I prayed. Hell, I was going to serve time. For what? Missing my wife and child. It rang. I shouldn't have taken that white man's ride. Our phone rang, but no answer. I didn't want to hang

up, 'cause all that awaited me was a jail cell. I knew they were timing me. I thought about pretending she'd answered and we were talking, because once I put down this phone, they'd have me for real. I pressed against the wall like I could melt into it, and escape. But no use.

No answer. "Alright," I said to myself. "Lock me up. Lock me the hell up. Y'all win. "

Alone in that cell, I thought I should have called the church or the Rev. or one of my family members. I should have called the plant or Bubs and Donnie. Maybe even Rev. Truesome. I hummed and sang songs, Marley, Rick James, *Burden Down, Lord*.

Guess I drifted off . . . dreamed I was out with an old lover but Laney and me were together, still married. My lover was drunk. We were out on the street, and my lover was tipsy, swaying and stumbling. I was holding her up, like I had Billy Reilly. She was dead weight, just like Reilly, and she stank like damp, musty old rags, but I held her. We were lost; I was lost, didn't know the way, and there were no names on the street signs. She vomited, and chewed-up food spilt all over my arms and hands, but I held on tight, to not let her fall. Then, the phone rang, from a corner phone booth across the street. I knew it was Delaney calling me, but I couldn't answer because I was holding up my lover, and she was clutching me tight, like Bill had, and if I let go, she'd fall on the hard, cold concrete. The phone rang, calling me, it was Laney, but I couldn't answer . . . Then, I dreamed Laney was kissing Bill Reilly. She was sitting on his lap, dabbing his forehead, kissing his face, attending to his wounds, saying how she loved him, *because I love white men. They treat me better than my husband ever could. He's black. Ignorant. Crude.* She sat on that white man's lap, kissing him, while I knelt on the floor of my jail cell, watching them, gripping cold, steel bars, unable to break free.

Barbershop talk—

"Heavy dream, man," Kwame said.

"Yeah. I know. When I awoke, I was still locked up. Just more afraid of losing her. I mean, Delaney was my dream woman. She was pretty and smart and a good lady. But there was never a time in our marriage when I wasn't out there like that, doing something I shouldn't of."

"Doing something, you mean, like cheating?"

"Naw, but not necessarily answering her call, being there for her."

"Too busy helping drunk womens in the street, huh, bruh?" Kwame laughed.

"Naw, the truth be told, I never felt we was gone make it. The day we finally decided to get married, we was living in a little apartment on Custer, just off Main Street. Laney and I were sitting in Delaware Park beneath a big tree, eating jerk chicken sandwiches she had picked up from a little Caribbean restaurant on Main. It was a sunny, Buffalo day, just enough wind so that I could inhale my baby, close my eyes and know she was next to me, from her scent. She was playing a cassette she said her college teacher had made for her. This was before I knew anything about Bill Reilly."

"You like reggae music?" She asked.

"It's alright."

"My college instructor made this, of Bob Marley and Peter Tosh. He's a white man, but he's pretty cool. She hit the play button and the music started. You know who Marley is, right?"

"Yeah, I know," I lied.

"You don't know a thing about this music, John, you're lying," she said, laughing, rocking to the beat from the box. All you know is James Brown and the Fabulous Flames," she laughed. "Rick James and all that funky stuff, she laughed. Funk man! Funky Buffalo Men—you and Rick!" She laughed.

She was dressed in jeans and a tank top, and I wanted to wrestle with my baby, hold her down, playful-like, and smother her with kisses, 'til we both laughed. But I knew she wouldn't like it."

"Rick's a bad boy," I said, trying to laugh along. "Buffalo's own!"

"Yeah, I know. Like you, Buffalo's own." She laughed, but I didn't.

We were beneath this big tree, where we could see the court, brothers bouncing balls like their lives were in the balance. Best basketball in Buffalo was at Delaware Park. Brothers skyin' high, snatching down the rock, and running up- court like the devil was behind 'em. Marley's song was *No Woman, No Cry*. I was kinda digging on the tune, but didn't wanna tell her. Didn't want to like music recommended to my woman by some white man. I wanted to leave my woman, run across the grass and bust into that game, to show her, show them, I could still hoop, that couldn't no white man ball like me. But there were some white boys, the best and baddest, who played at Delaware, too.

"Johnny, I'm expecting."

"Expecting what?"

"You know what, Silly," she said, rolling her eyes, touching my arm.

"You're pregnant?"

"Yes, we are."

"So that's what's been kicking in my gut."

"You mean in your bubble brain?" She smiled. "Yes, I'm carrying our baby now, and I want even more for us to make it. I want our family to be impregnable."

"Laney, I don't even know what that word means, but I want it too. Marry me." I rose to one knee, half up, half down.

"What it means is that I love you, John Smith. And I love this baby inside of me. So you know we're getting married. I knew that when I let you kiss me."

I wanted to say—*kiss?*—like I didn't believe her, but I did. She was like that, prissy and prim, but tough. Marley's jumpy-jump reggae beat made me want to dance with her; made me want to conquer frontiers for my baby. As I listened, it was like the music was saying one thing, and she was saying another: *No Woman, No Cry.* The music was telling me how tough it was gonna be, how we might not make it. Marley was warning me, I had to be different, not like those brothers across the way, skyin' toward baskets, but I didn't know how I could be anything else, anyone else, but a poor black man from cold-ass Buffalo.

"Maybe I'm not the man for you, Laney. You're too smart for me. Too intelligent, gonna go too far. Maybe you ought to be with somebody like a teacher or accountant or somebody. Somebody with more credentials or something."

"Johnny, I'm not going anywhere. And no, I'm not too intelligent for you, crazy man. We're just right. Soul mates."

Yeah, you are, and if you go on and get these degrees, why would you still want me?"

"Why wouldn't I? What would be different?"

"I wouldn't be good enough for you."

"You're not now," she laughed.

"I know. I know I'm not."

"Seriously, Knucklehead man, I love you."

She squeezed my hand. I liked this song: Marley. I believed him. But I wanted to believe her, too.

"Johnny," she said, "we help make one another good enough for the other. You make me more *good.* You make me better."

No Woman, No Cry. I wanted to cry, or flee, run over to that game and just be an ordinary black man, but how could I with a woman like her? She wanted me to be something more, but I just wanted to be like my brothas, just running over there. I was always gone be playing catch-up to white boys, and I knew I'd never catch up. The only thing I had on them was her and black skin. I just wanted to be black and ordinary, like them, and not like no white man, or trying to be. I wanted to sky to

the hoop and dunk, or hit a running jumper and high-five my brothas. I trusted that game, but not the game she was calling for, trying to compete with whitey, playing a different game on somebody else's court.

"Delaney, you're not hearing me," I said. "There are things I can never give you, things that you want, things a woman like you deserves."

"Like what, John?"

"Books, intellectual stuff, more money. Things that teacher gives you, I guess, or somebody smarter than me."

"Johnny Boy, just give me what you can."

"Delaney, I give you my soul."

Timeline:

Tuesday, October 14, 1980
A 37-year-old white lawyer, "TM," is stabbed to death by a black man on the corner of Pearl and West Chippewa. The witness, a black youth, E. Boyd, originally lies to police, telling them the assailant was white.

Johnny's Story, continued:

"Come on," I heard a voice say the next morning. "Get the hell up, Smith." I was half-asleep, because I hadn't really slept, but I rose up. As I followed the cop down the hall, I looked straight ahead and not inside the other cages, filled with other black brothers.

When I got to the front, there was Bill's woman, Amber, and a white man who looked like Reilly's twin—tall, bearded, wearing spectacles. Like Bill, he wore a white hippie's uniform: plaid shirt, jeans and funny-looking brown sandals with socks. Amber still looked hateful and mean, like she didn't wanna be there. The white dude was talking to the cops and gesturing. The cops were shaking their heads. After awhile, one of the cops walked away from the couple.

"Free to go," he said. "But your piece stays. Sign for your other belongings."

"Bill told us what happened," the look-alike said. "He kept insisting, 'he's innocent, he's innocent.' Bill's in the hospital now, but according to him, you saved his life."

"If I didn't cherish my Bill, he'd rot in here," Amber said, not to me or even to the other guy but kinda to herself, as though she was still working it through, wondering if I was just another black animal who should be locked up or dead. Maybe in their minds this killing spree was about that: extermination of the animals.

"He said they were beating him and you rescued him," the white guy said. "Bill said you saved his life." I later learned his name was Dennis Romanski, a friend of Bill and Amber, an attorney. He was going to represent me if needed, but first he was going to try to get all the charges dropped.

When I told the Dennis dude that I thought that I did have a permit for the gun, that I'd gotten it from my friend, Josh, he seemed to think that I'd be fine, and get off without any charges or time.

"Especially in light of the racial climate in Buffalo," Romanski said, "the cops are not trying to insight racial strife but instead lessen it, and in some ways, you're a hero."

Hero. I didn't believe it. And wasn't sure they did either, but I was glad Bill Reilly had lied to them. If he hadn't I might have rotted in that jail or got my ass beat by those cops. Dennis offered to drive me home, said it was best, "given the chaos in the streets," and I couldn't say no, even though I didn't want to ride in my neighborhood with these white people. Didn't want to be in the backseat of no white people's car. But I also didn't want to walk the streets or wait for the bus. She made me feel like I did with the cops; worse, because with her it was personal.

"Bill spent the night in the hospital for a precaution, but they're releasing him later today," Dennis said as we drove. "He told us what happened, that you didn't do it."

"He said that he was talking with you about your wife, that she had been frightened about the killer and therefore left for Canada," Amber said. "But why didn't you take him to a hospital?"

"Church was close. Everybody needs prayer."

"So was Deaconess Hospital," Amber said, her tone accusing me. I wanted to open the door and jump out at the first red light, but I knew I couldn't.

"Well, thank you," I said. "Those cops didn't want to let me go," I said. "They didn't believe me."

"I don't either," she said. "But I love my partner."

"There's been a lot of black backlash, violence against innocent whites, and they thought you were one such perpetrator," Dennis said.

"What did you want with Bill," she asked. "Why did you get in his car?"

"I just wanted to find my family," I said. "Besides, who is innocent anyway?"

"Good question," Dennis said. The car got quiet. She hated me. I had to play it cool or these white people could have me back in jail, for something. I was still in custody, really.

"Let me out here," I said to Romanski, when we got close to my home.

"Why?"

"Not safe for y'all on my block. They been stoning whites," I lied.

"We're armed," she said. Her voice said she wanted to shoot somebody, a nigger, like me.

Romanski pulled over fast, "out," he said. "Enough madness already," he said.

He sounded mad, at me, for not wanting them to take me all the way home. At her, for having a gun, and maybe at the insanity of innocent people no longer being innocent. Them, me—we was all crazy, all insane right now. All afraid, too.

"Thanks y'all," I said, throwing the door open and stepping out. I started walking fast, in the opposite direction from their car. I figured if she was gonna shoot me he'd have to first turn the car around. I was on Grider, down the block from the hospital where that strangling had happened. Hell, the .22-Caliber could hit me right now. He could come up behind me right now. I wished I still had my gun, so I began running, like they was after me. I was taking the long way home, so Amber and them couldn't follow me, so they wouldn't be sure where I was heading. I ran as fast as I could, long strides, missing the cracks in the sidewalk, but I didn't look down; I didn't need to. I'd missed that first crack getting out of their car. Now I had my rhythm. I was stretching out, like a chained dog that had broke loose. Or running a fast break with Bubs and Donny, and when I got to the goal, I was gonna dunk it. I ran through back alleys and backyards, leaped over fences, I didn't care. They wasn't gonna get me. I was a slave running to freedom, a black man running toward the sky.

When I approached our apartment, I slowed down and looked up; the white curtains were closed. Someone was there. Delaney liked the curtains shut and I never shut them, knew I had left them open. She was home. They were home.

I crept up the stairs quiet and fast, wanting to surprise them. I unlocked the door and opened it.

"Laney, Delaney Smith! Little Bit! Nisey! Denise!" No answer. The aroma hit me, chicken and sweet potatoes and good "Laney-Smells." I used to tease her, "Girl, you sure can cook! I just wanna be around you to smell and look!" I followed the smells into the kitchen. Nothing but aroma greeted me: no TV, none of Nisey's giggles, no complaining from Laney. The silence hit me. No Delaney, sitting at her table, ready to intimidate me, make me feel guilty. I was ready, but she wasn't here, but taped to the back of her usual chair was a note:

Johnny,

We came back. But you were gone, so we left. I closed the blinds. You need to keep them closed. First, I got a message from Mother Black at the church about you and some dirty, beaten, white man. Then I got a call from Bill Reilly, my old professor, well, from his wife. Something about you and a car and a gang and a gun. Something else about how you saved his life and Deliverance Church saved his soul but you're in trouble with the law. Or you were in trouble but he's going to fix it. Fix what? John, I was going to wait for you, to talk, but I can't take it.

I almost lost my religion and cursed her out. But Billy was my favorite teacher, so I told her I had left you and was just back here for our things and didn't care what the hell happened to your sorry behind.

But I do care. I don't know why; perhaps I need my head examined, and Nisey misses you so much.

Laney.

PS: Be safe, Crazy man.

I read it once more walking back to our bedroom. Then, I read it again, for clues. I sat on the bed, crumpled the note, opened it, read, and repeated those steps several times. I'd just missed them. Just like Laney, she'd cooked a meal for me . . . that Laney, I chuckled. But now what? Maybe I should just eat some food and wait. I had no appetite. I'd been starving in that jail; now I had food but didn't wanna eat. I laughed. What should I do? Where to look? Sitting on that bed, smelling that food, feeling lonely as hell, I laughed 'til I cried, then I just slid down to my knees.

Timeline: Friday,

October 17, 1980

Two Kensignton station police officers bring a peaceful end to a potentially volatile situation when a black man carrying a pellet gun momentarily pulls the weapon on them. The officers say that they could have legally fired on the suspect, but hesitate to do so, partially because of the mounting racial tensions in the city because of the six .22-caliber killings. Their restraint is wise, given the powder keg that is the city of Buffalo.

Chapter Ten

Timeline:

Sunday, October 19, 1980
An estimated 5,000 Western New Yorkers jam Niagara Square for a Unity Day rally. Blacks, whites, Hispanics, and others are in attendance, with more than 200 organizations taking part. An interracial Central City Choir sings songs, including the Civil Rights anthem, *We Shall Overcome*. Speakers call for love, unity, peace and an end to racial strife.

At the rally, Black leaders announce that they want Attorney General Benjamin Civiletti to take charge of the investigation. Rev. Charles Fisher, III, of BUILD, urges Civiletti to "come here to oversee this investigation and stay here until this killer is caught."

Catholic Bishop Edward Head exhorts those in attendance to be "men and women of healing and vision."

Rabbi Sholom Stern asks, "How many disasters do we have to endure to realize that when one group is attacked, discriminated against, and murdered, we all are potential victims?"

Labor leader, George Wessel, of the AFL-CIO, proclaims the following: *Three years ago [1977] we had a bad storm in Buffalo and the whole world knew about it. I just hope the whole world knows about today, Unity Day in Buffalo.*

And, a day later, Ray Hill's passionate column on Buffalo's Unity Day Rally begins with the headline, *The City Proclaims Its Unity in Defying a Madman's Assault.*

Barbershop talk—

"I was at that Unity Rally, man. It was cold, but you felt warm and hopeful, like maybe Buffalo was gone change over what had happened," Kwame said.

"Kwam, I don't know what I was doin' that day, Johnny said. "But I guess I was with y'all in spirit."

"I was in Ohio."

"We know, Eddie, we know."

"But, man, I would have loved to have been here just to feel what it was like. My sister and mom said, don't come home. Too dangerous."

"It was scary. You looked at every white man as a possible assailant," Kwame said.

"Maybe that's how they look at us when they cross the street or white women clutch their purses and walk faster whenever we're nearby ..."

I loved the way Bridgette looked at me, the way she tilted her head when sleepy. The way her glasses fell down over her nose. I loved her shape, the way jeans fit her firm thighs and small, tight waist. She'd battled weight problems since adolescence, and she was winning.

"Even though I love my sweets," she said. I loved the mom she was—determined to make her son something special.

"President, maybe," she said.

"But he wants to play ball."

"Rhodes Scholar," she said. "He'll go to Oxford, after his Ivy League days are done."

"And then what?"

"The presidency!"

We'd met a Women's Jazz concert downtown, I was standing beside a tree, and she was in front of me in a lawn chair, shaking her head to the band. It was a quartet of ladies—two white, two black: keyboard, sax, guitar and drums. They were covering a Kirk Whalum song, *Unconditional*, I think it was. I knew it was Whalum, and the sister in the lawn chair smiled back at me, with a look that said, *I know you're enjoying this as much as me, but why won't you dance, why won't you swing?* How could I tell her that I swung on the inside? So I gave her the thumbs-up sign. After the concert was over, I walked over to her, and we talked. We dated the following Friday: Dinner, a long walk at night, and a long talk in my car, outside her house, once I drove her home.

Her mother was black, her dad, white. They'd been married, but not for long. Her dad had died, car accident, when she was little, two years old. "I imagined they had a fairy-tale romance. My dad was a dashing knight and my mom a fair maiden. But I think they were very alone. My dad's family didn't accept mom. I don't really know any of them, my dad's side. I could try, but I don't. I think maybe I should now that I have A.B., especially since his dad is white, too. But I don't know, I just don't want them to reject him."

I wanted to hold her that night, to get her. Her green eyes drew me. Her lightness against the dark night, drew me. The way she walked, slightly slumped over, but tall, like she'd always carried loads.

I wanted her to know, *I will help you carry it.* I wanted her to trust me, let me inside those drowsy eyes, behind them. At some point, as we talked, my arm wrapped around her and she lay her head on my shoulder. I wanted to lie with her, cuddle, so close we would sleep and dream the

same dream. We'd wake up lovers, and I would never leave. She'd want me forever. But I'd been through too many women. I'd carried too much pain, burial and fear, to have a *dream woman*—that was for kids like her son. I was too cynical, too sacred. I didn't trust happiness, a line from a movie I once saw. But I knew that first night, I could love her, and I wanted her to be my friend.

Near the end of the date, she asked me, "Edward, what do you want, and what are the boundaries?"

My mind said, "I don't know." My mind said, "All I want is to hold you." I wanted to undress her, slowly, take off her blue jeans. Take off her pink t-shirt. I wanted her to be seated, not standing, as she was right now. We stood, facing each other, beneath a street lamp. Our cars were parked beside one another. We stood in the aisle between them. I wanted her to sit up on her car, and allow me to massage her feet. I wanted to brush her hair back so she'd close her eyes and hum with my heart. I wanted to take off her glasses, so she could close her eyes and see me clearer.

"Bridgette, may I call you Bridge? That's my first question."

Her look said "yes," so I continued. "Bridge, I want peace with God and myself. And no boundaries. I don't want boundaries with you."

Her look said, "okay." I pulled her close and closed my eyes.

Timeline:

November/December, 1980:
In November, Buffalo law officials meet with those in Atlanta to compare notes. Both cities are working on cases involving serial killers of blacks. Atlanta authorities have been searching for over a year to solve the murders or disappearances of 14 black children, mainly young males.

The reward for the killer eventually reaches $100,000, with the City of Buffalo, Erie County, and the Chamber of Commerce each contributing $25,000.

In December, there are no new leads in the case, in spite of the questioning of more than 1,500 area residents.

Frustrated, blacks call for a Christmas boycott of Buffalo's downtown stores, in protest of the city's handling of the case.

Johnny's Story, continued:

I couldn't sleep, so after awhile, I got down on my knees and prayed. Praying, all of them songs was mixed up in my head. Bob Marley, singin' *No Woman, No Cry*. Delaney's church choir singin', *Climbing Up the Mountain*. Didn't the old folks sing, *He'll make a way out of no way?* Well,

I was at *no way*, and didn't know how to climb that mountain and find a way. I was on my knees for hours, prayin' and thinkin' and lookin' at the four walls, pictures of Laney and me and Baby Girl. I was on my knees for so long, they hurt, but I figured God might bless me if I earned it.

"Good Lord, I need your help. My family's gone, and they killing us, Lord. I don't want to die, now. But being alone like this, is worse, Lord. I need you. Give me strength, Man, cause You are Everything."

I prayed some more, but after that, I just stayed on my knees, listening for God's voice. But all I heard was music, Ricky James singin' *You and I*, and voices, speaking. But I couldn't make out the voices. It was like they was them unknown tongues, like in Laney's church. I wanted to understand those voices. Heck, I wanted to dance to the music. Wanted to pray some more. I was supposed to be doing something, help find this killer, help my friends organize, something. Another one of them church songs was in my head, Laney's choir singing, *Lord don't move that stumbling block. Give me the strength to climb.* But the choir was them kids who'd stomped Billy Reilly. They was dressed in black and white robes, singing and laughing. I got up off my knees. The Imani, House of Peace, was a long run, but I knew I could make it, just thinking 'bout my babies would keep me going, running up those mountains.

Timeline:

December, 1980
Just before Christmas, the killing spree turns to New York City. All of the attacks in NYC occur in the space of a day, Dec 22nd:

Johnny Adams, 25, narrowly escapes death when he is knifed by a white assailant around 11:30 a.m.

Around 1:30 p.m., Ivan Frazer, 33, is attacked, deflecting the knife blade with his hand, and then fleeing on foot.

The next four victims are less fortunate: around 3:30 p.m., a dark-skinned Hispanic male, Luis Rodriguez, 19, is stabbed to death in Manhattan.

No motive is suggested in the deaths of 30-year-old Antone Davis, knifed around 6:50 p.m. or 20-year-old Richard Renner, killed a few hours later.

The last victim, discovered just before midnight, a black "John Doe," is stabbed to death on the street near Madison Square Garden. For the New York City slayings, the killer is labeled the Mid-town Slasher, because all of the victims were knifed to death. As mentioned, three of them were black males, and the fourth was a dark-skinned Hispanic male. Witnesses to the New York City slayings say that that killer wore gold-rimmed

glasses, was muscular and weighed about 160-170 pounds. They describe him as about 5 feet, 7 inches tall and about 40 years old.

Buffalo officials are interested in the Manhattan slayings due to the *striking similarities* of the cases, one official noting that all the cases are linked by *a common thread of brazenness and randomness*. The Buffalo area task force enters *phase two* of the investigation, characterized as *a second, analytical stage* by law enforcement officials, as they use computers to re-sort and reanalyze data. The task force itself is now about 35 in number.

Timeline:

After Christmas, the killing continues, as though the assassin took a holiday from mayhem.

December 29, 1980 to January 1, 1981
Two more black men, in Buffalo and Rochester, are stabbed to death. Roger Adams, 31, is stabbed to death in Buffalo on Dec. 29. And Wendell Barnes, 26, is stabbed to death in Rochester on December 30. Albert Menefee, 32, of Buffalo, survives a stabbing attack on December 31st, the knife thrust nicking his heart. On January 1st, Larry Little and Calvin Crippen survive separate attacks, each fighting off his white assailant.

Also, in December, in the Buffalo area, a local neo-Nazi group announces its plans to hold its own rally downtown, near City Hall, on January 15, 1981, the anniversary of Dr. King's birth.

Chapter Eleven

Johnny's Story, continued:

I ran to the Imani, but it was locked. Nobody was there. So I ran through the streets of the city, 'til my knees hurt, and I was winded. I never found them. Delaney had moved to Rochester, to live with her friend, Renee, and her two kids. I didn't know that for weeks, though. Only thing kept me sane 'til I found that out was, killer wasn't studin' bout nobody but brothas, ya know? So I hoped my girls was safe.

Delaney and me was split up, for about three years. First, I left Buffalo, moved around some, went down to Tennessee to see my people's land, and lived there for some months, after 'Laney and me split up. Too much pain here in the Nickel. I wanted to stay in Tennessee, but not alone. So I came back and got a job in Lockport, watched my daughter grow up on weekends and holidays, all the while trying to convince my baby I was a changed man.

"So why didn't you stay in Tennessee, why'd you come back? I mean, your family could've moved down there."

"Yeah, they coulda, and maybe woulda, but there's only so many places you can call home and this is it for me."

Timeline:

January 18, 1981
Joseph Christopher, 25, a white Army private from Buffalo, is arrested at Fort Benning, GA, following a knife attack on a fellow soldier. According to army reports, on this day, Christoper gets into an argument with a black recruit in the barracks, attempting to murder him with a paring knife. While in the stockade, Christopher cuts himself in the groin with a razor and is sent to the base hospital.

Fort Benning officials alert Buffalo homicide detectives that two Army nurses in the Fort Benning Hospital overhear Joseph Christopher claim that he *had killed some Black men up North.*

April, 1981
A search of Christopher's former residence turns up quantities of .22-caliber ammo, a gun barrel and two sawed-off rifle stocks. A check of Christopher's whereabouts during the previous year, 1980, shows that he had enlisted in the Army on November 13th, in Buffalo, arrived at Ft. Benning on November 19th, and taken a leave on December 19th,

returning January 4th. The police also find a bus ticket verifying his arrival in New York City on December 20th.

Johnny's Story, continued:

We were separated 'til about '84. Eventually, I got a job, driving buses for NFT. Reason Laney didn't come back right away, was I guess she was afraid I would mess up again. Maybe I didn't show her I loved her enough. Not sure I knew how. I was jealous of anybody, like that white teacher, who could give her something I couldn't. Who I thought fulfilled her idea of *man* more than I did. Guess I had to learn that what I had was enough. Hard ass lesson to learn. Hell, I was jealous and possessive and insecure. She was my jewel, but I couldn't tell her, for fear she'd know. Couldn't cherish her like I do now. I was too much of a punk, afraid of being punked. So I punked my own damn self. Guess I was like every other funky-ass brotha, too funked up to love a woman right. But then, one day, I told myself, *you can try.* I told myself, *all in, or all out.* And I ain't never been all in with her. So I told her that I was gone love her the only way I can love, and hope that that's enough.

Johnny rose, surveying the barbershop. Watching him, I felt like Marley was looking down on us, Robeson, Malcolm, that they'd been in on our conversations, too.

"What we did here, needs to keep going. Get your book out, get it published or whatever, Eddie, man. Don't let 'em stop you," Kwame said, reading my mind.

"Yeah, just speak the truth in love," Johnny said.

"You sound like a preacher, I said."

"Laney thinks I got *The Call* to preach," he grinned.

Timeline: April, 1981

Joseph Christopher's extradition to Buffalo is front-page news. The short, spectacled, white young man is shown on the front pages of the papers. His trial is front-page news. Family members of the deceased are interviewed, pleading for justice, finally. Christopher is indicted, charged with separate counts of second-degree murder in the deaths of Glenn Dunn, Harold Green, and Emmanual Thomas, with a fourth murder count, of Joseph McCoy, added to the list on June 29. All of the victims were shot with a sawed-off .22-caliber Ruger rifle. Ballistics tests link casings found at the scenes of the slayings to Ruger ammunition and other material seized during a search of Christopher's home. He is never charged with the death of McCoy or the two cab drivers.

Timeline: Monday, May 11, 1981
Bob Marley dies.
Robert Nesta Marley is 36 years old when he succumbs to cancer in a hospital in Miami, Florida.

The same day:
Joseph G. Christopher, his head covered with a gray ski mask and his hands and feet manacled, is escorted to his arraignment. Christopher pleads "not guilty."

The victims' families express grief, anger and a sense of relief at news of the capture and the charges.

Dunn's mother says, "I read the 23rd Psalm and I go to church. I know the Lord says vengeance is mine. I know the Bible says we shouldn't hate. But Lord help me, "I hate him. I hate him. I hate him!"

She continues, "At first, I wanted to go out and get revenge on every white person I saw. But I know I can't blame all white people for what one did . . . Now that they've caught him, my son can rest in peace. I'm glad they caught him, and I hope he gets what he deserves. It had gotten to the point where I couldn't sit in a car without worrying."

Thomas' wife utters similar sentiments when interviewed by reporters, explaining how the couple's young daughters "were so attached to him [their father]. He used to take them on outings . . . [T]his summer, I know they'll be sitting on that front porch waiting for him to take them out. . . ."

Of the man accused of the murder of her husband, she remarks, "I'm gonna be there [in the courtroom] . . . I know I probably won't be able to take it, but I want to look at him. I just want to see him."

Barbershop talk—

"What I don't understand is this, why didn't this case receive more attention, from anybody, from black or white people? Thirteen men were murdered by this crazed killer, but I dare you to find a record of it outside of a few newspaper accounts in Buffalo and New York City. Most people don't even know it happened."

"Yeah, if this says anything it's like our lives weren't even worth the newsprint," Johnny said. "It's like they were invisible men."

"Black man in America, what you think? Kwame said. "A war on black men waged out in the streets. And nobody seemed to care. Still don't."

So one is left to wonder if the lack of attention was due to the fact that the killings were of brothers or in Buffalo, or both?" I asked.

"I wonder that too," Johnny said.

Timeline:

May 12, 1981
In Buffalo, Christopher is under the tightest security and is placed in custody without bail. Christopher wants to represent himself, refusing to be represented by the lawyers retained by his widowed mother. He also refuses psychiatric examination. A fourth murder count is added to the list on June 29th, plus charges related to non-fatal Buffalo stabbings in December and January.

There were more than 2,000 suspects in the seven-month .22 caliber killings manhunt. But Joseph Christopher wasn't one of them. Those who know him characterize him as "a quiet young man," one who was "a good kid." At Burgard High School, where he attended, prior to dropping out during his junior year, Christopher was characterized as "a quiet kid that you really wouldn't notice." In the Army, they remembered him as a quiet recruit who read the Bible.

Three witnesses to fatal stabbings in New York City identify Joseph Christopher. In New York City, indictments against Christopher are returned in the murder of Luis Rodriguez and the non-fatal stabbing of Ivan Frazier.

Barbershop talk—

Listening, looking at the barbershop walls, I was sorry our nightly sessions were about over. I had to return to Ohio, to teach. School started back soon.

"Johnny, Kwame," I said, "I just want people to be able to study all of this, the confusion and chaos, black men dying, white people getting beaten, the politicians and leaders who came to town, Rev. Jesse Jackson, George Bush, Sr. It was a concentrated racial nightmare, that nobody knows about, and I want people, black people, white people, to know this history and to see how one city, our city, dealt with it."

"Eddie, man, I don't know about all that," Johnny said. "I just wanted to get it out. It's been bottled up inside for years, and I needed to tell somebody."

"Just couldn't keep it to yourself, huh, Preacher?" Kwame said.

"Yeah, something like that," Johnny said, "and don't y'all forget, we also got the Black Leadership Forum out of this."

"That's a group of black Buffalo leaders that meet every other Saturday, right?"

"Yeah, Eddie, man, and it started back in 1980 as a response to the .22-Caliber."

"Hell, but it always takes that," Kwame said, "for us black folks to try and unite."

"Yeah," Johnny and I said in unison.

"See you soon," was the email I had sent Bridgette. I'd added, "You're my Bridge, and I love you." It was corny, but I'd been saying it for years, and she liked it.

Giving her what she liked, what she wanted, was how we'd coped. Paying her bills, helping raise her son, but A.B. and I didn't speak anymore. When I got back there, we would have it out, one way or another. Guess I could kick his ass, or he, mine. I could chastise him like the dad I wasn't. Or I could just let his ass go. Right now, I had chosen the latter.

"When?" was her first word when I called.

"Can't say hello?"

"When are you coming?"

"Why, you got a man staying in my crib now and gotta get him out?"

"Maybe." She paused, "No, I just want to be able to prepare Anderson for your coming. He still loves you, but you hurt him. Says he doesn't want you back."

"Then he can leave."

"And go where, Edward? He says he wants to join the service when he's old enough, says there's a recruiter comes to the high school that he's friends with."

"With whom he's friends," I corrected. I hated when she called me Edward, no longer calling me Eddie.

"Right, whatever. The only reason I asked was so I can tell him you're coming, and please don't disappoint him and say you're coming and not come, Ed."

"Let me get this straight, he can't stand me, doesn't want me coming back ever, but if I say I am coming and don't come then I might hurt his feelings? Is that right?"

"Yes. You don't understand."

"I guess I don't."

Timeline:

October, 1981
Christopher waives his right to a jury trial in Buffalo, placing his fate in the hands of a judge. Months later, he was found mentally incompetent for trial, but the ruling was later reversed. On April 27, 1982, he is convicted on three-counts of first-degree murder, drawing a prison term of 60 years to life.

Barbershop talk—

A white guy was at the door, knocking on the glass, like somebody was after him, like he'd break it if he wasn't let in.

"That's Reilly," Johnny said, looking at the man on the outside. Johnny was seated at the back of the shop, at one of the chess tables.

Kwame opened the door, and the white man walked in.

He stood in the doorway like he was frightened. He and Johnny just stared at each other. Then Johnny looked back down at the chess pieces before him, presumably playing a chess game against himself.

"What the hell you doin' here?" Johnny asked, not looking up from the board. Reilly was dressed in a long, black, heavy trench coat, and he kept his hands in his pockets. I wondered if he was packing.

"John, I was told about a story in the works. I wanted to see if I could help, lend a hand."

"I done forgot my manners. Bill, this is Kwame, the shop owner, and that there is the Doc, named Eddie. And now, you can leave on out that door. This ain't your story, Bill," Johnny said, knocking over a white pawn with his black queen. "Never was, and it never will be. Kwame, kick his ass out of here, before I do."

Reilly was backed up against the door, like he wondered if this was going to be a repeat of what happened to him years ago. His eyes bulged, big and white; another gang of black men and him, alone. But he'd come to us.

"I just heard someone was working on telling the story of . . ."

"Of what?" Johnny interrupted him, then he leaped up out of his chair, slammed Reilly up against the wall and held him there. "Ain't nothing you can say or add, Professor! Whatever you been studying or trying to do about black folks, go do it somewhere else, man! Besides, how you find out about us anyway?"

"Your wife . . ."

"My wife?" Johnny punched him hard, in the gut. Bill doubled over, and Kwame grabbed John and pulled him away.

Kwame stood between the two of them. "What's going on here?"

"Ain't nobody invite his ass," Johnny said. "I'm not your brother, white man, neither your friend."

"Then what are you to me, John?" Reilly was coughing from the punch, but he eyes said there was no retaliation. "What are you to me? Your wife ran into my wife at the mall, and Delaney mentioned a professor . . . you, sir," he said, looking at me, "was working on the story."

Chapter Twelve

Timeline:

September, 1983

Christopher sits for an interview with Buffalo journalists, estimating that his murder spree had claimed a minimum of thirteen lives. Reporters note that he does not deny the murders of Parler Edwards and Ernest Jones, but no charges are ever filed on those cases. In July, 1985, Christopher's Buffalo conviction was overturned on grounds that the judge had improperly barred testimony which pointed toward Christopher's mental incompetence. Three months later, in Manhattan, a jury rejects Christoper's insanity plea, convicting him in the murder of Rodriguez and the wounding of Ivan Frazier.

Barbershop talk—

The day after Reilly came around, Johnny was still hot.

"That pissed me off," he said, "him showing up here like that. Can't we have anything to ourselves? But Bill done stuck to his story, all these years, never ratted me out, not even to his missus, far as I can tell."

"And his story is also yours, my friend, in some ways."

"Yeah, it is. But I ain't done, y'all. I'm still angry, not just at Bill, but at white people in general. Sometimes, I still say under my breath, 'I hate white people. I hate 'em.'"

"We all say that," I said.

"'Cause it's war," Kwame said.

"And it's never not war," Johnny said, "even when it seems to be peace."

"Maybe the nature of the warfare, the battle just changes," I said.

"You right, Eddie, man. And sometimes, I used to think I was just gone be a casualty, just another brother all messed up in the head and in his life. One while, I really didn't think me and Laney was gone make it, even after we reconciled, 'cause I had too much anger at white folks, at the system. Hell, even at myself, for not being white."

"You mean, for not being 'right,'" Kwame chuckled. We joined in, all recalling the adage, white is right, and black, get back.

"So, John, when did you know?" I asked.

"When?" He smiled.

"One day, I knew it was right, like I heard music in my head, God telling me: 'this is it, boy. You got it.' It was one of those sunny late summer days we get in Buffalo make you glad you live here, forget all that winter snow. We was all in Delaware Park, our first time going to the park after we reconciled. I remember it cause I would never take Baby Girl to that park, to any park, like I was afraid that the killer was still on the loose and might shoot her, trying to hit me. I was afraid of the ghosts. Anyhow, Nisey was riding her new bike. I'm watching so nobody touches Baby Girl. This was her first bike, and I'd told her, 'no training wheels. You going straight for the big time.' At first, I walked alongside her, holding onto the bike as she rode, but after awhile, I said, 'You got the hang of it, Nisey, so it's time for me to let go.'

"'You sure I can do this, Daddy?'

"'You my Baby Girl, ain't you?'

"'Always, my daddy,' she said, and I let go.

"First she was a little wobbly, but I could tell she wasn't gone fall, and Laney and me were gone watch her like hawks, just in case. She started riding and after a couple of times of starting and stopping, but not tipping over, she rode past our bench yelling, 'Look, daddy. Look mommy!'

"Nisey was going pretty fast and straight, so I released Delaney's hand, stood up from that park bench and waved.

"'What you thinking, Johnny?' Delaney, asked as we both watched and waved, too.

"'What I'm thinking, Laney?' I looked at my wife.

"'Yes, John Smith, what are you thinking?'

'How good God is.'"

Timeline:

1993

Joseph Christopher dies in prison, of lung cancer in 1993. Several local papers mention the death of this maniac. Otherwise, his death, like his killing spree, was fairly obscure, except in Western New York.

Christopher's aim had been to start a race war between blacks and whites, and in Buffalo, New York, our hometown, he'd nearly succeeded.

Chapter Thirteen

Our barbershop sessions were done.

I'd seen all the relatives I could, William, Mark, Rose, and I'd been to the Falls a couple of times, and also Toronto, one of my favorite cities. I was leaving today. A few years back, I was driving back home every other weekend, 400 miles, to care for my parents. They were now deceased: mom, Alzheimer's and dad, cancer. Though I didn't come that often anymore, the drive was auto-pilot; take the 33 east to the I-90, west and south, out of the city, toward Erie, PA, and Ohio. I didn't want to leave, but I had to. I had Bridgette and A.B. and work in Ohio, obligations. But the woman and I cried all the time, inside, and the kid couldn't stand me. *No woman, no cry*. No kid, no cry. I wanted to stay longer, go through old neighborhoods one more time, visit dad's grave, or see the Falls one last time. I wanted to cry, shout or just be free. If I returned, when I returned, could Bridgette and I ever really make our relationship what it should be? For each of us? Driving, I was listening to Buffalo's own Grover Washington blast out "Mr. Magic," one of his signature songs, when I turned off my course and took the 290, toward the University, my alma mater.

Bill was in his office, his door open, typing. He looked up from his computer screen.

"Hey, sit down," he said, "I'll be right with you. Let me finish this sentence."

"Okay."

His office was small, cluttered with papers, books, and a futon, as though he lived, slept here, and cleaned up once a semester. It reminded me of my own office. Like with mine, I imagined it held old, graded essays never retrieved by fleeing students. And, good profs that we were, and cautious, we dared not toss them, just in case, years later, they came back—*Change my grade*— *I didn't deserve this*—*I deserved something higher*—Please, for us, revise history, and make things better. On his desk was also what I took to be a family photo, of him, a woman and a boy. I thought of the slain boy, Glenn Dunn. Several African masks stared at me from one wall, and abstract paintings graced the other walls, lines and streaks open to interpretation

I began, even though his fingers still spoke to the keys. "I could use your eyes and memory," I said.

His fingers answered back. *Tap-tap, tap-tap, tap-tap, tap-tap-tap*.

"I could use your eyes and memory," I said again, louder, and his typing ceased. He wheeled his chair from behind the monitor and I looked into his eyes. I saw fear, white fear, the kind I got when I entered an elevator and a lone white woman, already there, looked up at me, envisioning the black male monster, the myth. I wondered what Bill envisioned, and why he seemed to venture into blackness.

"Bill, you know the story, and I could use a trained and critical eye on the manuscript, before I submit it. I'd like your help. I'm on my way back to Ohio, but I thought I'd take the chance and solicit your help down the road."

"Edward, I know it's an important story," he said. "But I want no part of it. It's yours and Johnny's and Kwame's, not mine. It's for blacks to tell. John was right."

"Yes, and it's important that I get it out, that it be published, that it not become some obscure tale known to fewer and fewer people."

He reached behind his monitor and drank from a cup, of coffee, I guessed.

"Well, if I thought people wanted to read about the killing spree and its effect on this city, I would have written about it years ago, from the perspective of my own experiences, but I do believe that they wanted it buried, like that miscreant who perpetrated the spree. City of Good Neighbors, you know?"

"But don't people need to know? Or, more precisely, don't people need to not forget?" Saying that, I wondered if, like Johnny, he'd almost been a casualty. I wondered if this white man had scars. Or, had they healed? "Aren't we, as teachers and scholars, duty bound to research and read and write about historical occurrences?"

"Some we are, and we aren't. And, really, I must get going. We live in Grand Island, so I have a long commute. I don't talk about that period in my life anymore," he said, standing up at his desk. "I think it was a lapse in judgment for me to come to the barbershop."

"Okay," and I rose to go, pushing one of his books, which was falling off his desk, back onto the firm surface. "Maybe it's what Johnny says. It's like you're bound together, but there's a wall between you nonetheless. And the rope that binds you, you wonder how it goes over or under the wall. You're on one side, and I'm on the other, you know?"

"Yes, I know. That's why I ventured. And that, well, never mind, but each time I tuck O'Neil into bed . . . "

"O'Neil?"

"Yes, our son, named after Buck. A great man. O'Neil is now ten years old. We started late." He coughed. "But I think about racial matters each

time I tuck our boy into bed or say his name. Maybe that was my way of trying to bridge the racial gulf, a distance I have, frankly, given up trying to cross."

"So you've given up, but you're trying to signify that racial crossing through your son's name?"

"Yes, through any means necessary, isn't that how it goes?"

"That's crazy. Race is all around us, man, choking us. So here you are, trying to accomplish some kind of racial reconciliation, but then, you're not. That's crazy," I said, moving toward the door.

"No more insane, or crazy, than what happened here, or has happened elsewhere in terms of matters of race." Behind him, the African masks hung, implacable, and resolute.

"With all you did, and perhaps have done, you haven't done enough. You're sad, man. I'm ashamed of you."

"And I'm ashamed of your people."

"Why?"

"The way you let yourselves down. Your people, like Buck O'Neil, are the most heroic on the face of the globe. They, clearly, possess grace under pressure. Yet, paradoxically they seem the most perplexed."

"Yeah, I know, doc, I know. So where does that leave us?"

"At an impasse." He stood, walked toward me, and offered his hand. "I have a contact at Cornell who might be of some service in terms of publishing your work."

"Thanks. I'll send it soon." But saying that, I knew I didn't want his help, and probably wouldn't send it. That would make me like Johnny and any other black man, needing the aid of the white man he loathed. And I didn't want to need this cat, ever. "Thanks. Look for it in about a week or so," I lied.

"You're welcome. Be safe."

"You too, Bill. Peace."

Outside, the temperature seemed to have dropped. It was colder, more windy. Maybe publishing this piece would be even harder than with my first book. Reilly had offered to do what I'd hoped but I didn't want his help, the white man's sanction or approval, though I guessed I needed it. Damn. But wasn't that who I was writing for? Or was it for my sorry black brothers and sisters who made me ashamed, too? Maybe the men who died would have made me ashamed. That boy was sitting in a stolen car when he was killed. He might have grown up just another black mf'ing thug. His children's children, the same. None of them were wealthy; they were mostly black and poor and ignorant, living from check to check, working the swing shift, or the streetcorner, just to make ends. What would they have become? What had I become?

I had already failed Anderson Black Anderson. Kid could pass for white, but he wanted to be called *Black*. What did I want? No boundaries, even though there always were, even for white guys like Bill, or the almost white, like A.B. Whether I liked it or not, he was mine, and so was she.

"When you make love with a woman, when you have sex with her, you give her a piece of you that you never get back," Kwame had said.

She had pieces of me inside. I had pieces of her inside. I was hers, whether it made sense or not. "Let's get married," I could say that to her, I guessed. Do the damn thing. I felt obligated.

I started the car, turned on the stereo; Buffalo's own, Rick James, *Bustin Out (On Funk)*. The music surrounded me, like those young brothers had encircled Bill. The funky sound pounded the air, like their fists had his face. What were his wounds? What were mine? The sound, the speed, my foot on the pedal, my hands on the wheel. My manscript, Bill's books, and his son with a wise black man's name. Maybe I should turn around and kick his ass. Maybe I should beg forgiveness. Or ask him to be my friend. My real friend. Maybe I should stop by Kwame's one more time, to sort it all out, listening and talking with brothers. Or drive by dad's gravesite, and speak to him, but I'd cry, for dad and myself, and Johnny and Kwame and Rick James and Grover Washington and all the dead brothers. I'd cry and kneel on the ground, and pray. I'd cry for Bill, too. He had scars, too. Maybe white men, white people, could be invisible too. There he was, wanting to help black people, to do the right thing, but he couldn't. His race trapped him, and Amber, too, I guessed. Naw, I needed to leave now, or I'd be trapped, too, like I felt with Bridge and A.B., but I'd have to leave Buffalo, eventually. Besides, I'd be no less sad, whenever I left, or wherever I traveled. The grey sky held no answers. The black road ahead whispered nothing, just miles and music, as the long drive *back home*, loomed ahead. But like Johnny had said, *only so many places you can call home*. Bridge wanted to be my home. She had given me her son, and her heart. The 22-caliber killer cut out black men's hearts. Could I cut out mine? And give it to her? And, would she accept? I did not know.

I turned up my music, blasting it even louder, wanting to hold onto something from Buffalo, so I blasted Ricky James, and sung along with the sounds. I exited the highway. Took a left at the light. Took the highway in the opposite direction. I began driving, not south, toward Ohio, and *home*, but north, toward the Falls and Canada. Once I crossed over the Peace Bridge, I would call her. Bridge. Once I crossed that boundary, I'd know.

Black Messiahs Die

Black Messiahs Die

. . . The young men shall utterly fall (Isaiah 40: 30)

"What can we get for his life?"— someone in the huddle of men asked. They stood across from her desk, speaking in whispers.

"Not sure, several million at least, but how the hell didn't that cop recognize the kid? He's featured on every TV show and magazine cover, and was worth 100 million?" Cassinelli shook his head, his blond ponytail swinging like the tail of a dog.

"Dan, 100 mil's — conservative. He was a gold mine for years to come," Coach Sasser said.

"Decades," Rudolph added, "the shoe deal, the other endorsements . . ." his voice trailing off, as he noticed Eden staring at them, as opposed to typing the sports agency's statement about Jonathan's slaying.

O

"So, girl, what you wanna do?" Jonathan asked, dropping keys on her desk.

Here he was again, manchild in the promised land, like in the books in the black lit class, Bigger Thomas with a jumpshot, rich because he could leap and smile. Jonathan's smile was mesmerizing, *just the thing for commercials and television spots*, according to the agents: perfect white teeth set against smooth black skin. A bandanna beneath his baseball cap, tilted just-so and big diamonds in each ear, he sauntered into the agents' offices — Cassinelli, Rudolph and Associates, Attorneys at Law. Thick platinum chains hung the initials, *J G*, across his chest, and he daily sported the newest hip-hop gear and sneakers. *Size 14*, he'd say, winking as he raised a foot to show off a sneak when passing her desk. Today, he was decked out in blue.

"*Carolina Blue*, baby, just like Jordan, but you know I'm going straight to the show. But if I was playing college ball, I'd be wearin' these for sho'."

Jonathan was right; he'd been recruited by the top college basketball programs in the country. According to the scouts and the Coach, he was that good, able to write his own ticket; in this case, go straight from high school to the NBA, his future assured by a forty-inch vertical leap and a jump shot.

Eden focused on her text. "Jonathan, I'm on break, studying for the Bar Exam. You know what it is, correct?"

"Yeah, I know. I used to wanna be a lawyer too, 'til . . ."

"'Til what?"

"'Til 'bout the sixth, seventh grade, when school got hard . . . and basketball got easy."

"That's nice."

"Hey, let's us go for a ride," he asked, picking up his keys and dangling them before her so the Mercedes Benz logo swung like a pendulum. "Let's just go for a ride. We can drive on up to Xenia to see your peeps." Looking down at her, he flashed the TV grin groomed for interviews and press conferences.

"Jonathan, I have to study. This is my break time." Looking up, Eden placed her book down.

"Looks difficult."

"It's not easy, but one day I want my own agency."

"Representing lady jocks, huh?"

"Representing anyone."

"Once I sign, how 'bout you come work for me? Mr. Cass and 'nem say I'ma be bout worth 90, 100 mil with endorsements and all. Gonna need a special assistant," he said, the large diamonds in his ears twinkling like stars. "What you think?"

"I think, Jonathan . . . no, I know, I'm not in law school to become your special assistant."

"You working at a sports agency, ain't you?"

"But . . . " she said, staring at her book and the papers on her desk.

"What you don't understand, Eden," he said, turning her book so the title faced him, "is when I get my money, I'm gone need somebody I can trust." He picked up her book.

"And now you want to read my law books?"

"Yeah. Tax Law? Lemme check it out when you finished, okay?"

"Jonathan, let me get this straight. You don't carry any school books. You don't seem to ever study and you want to read my law school text?"

"Yeah, cuz I'ma need to know how to handle my money when I get paid," he said, emphasizing the word "paid," as though she didn't know what a top-three draft pick was worth.

"Jonathan, you *never* carry books. Are you still in school?"

"Yup," he said, raising up to his full height, 6'9" and looking at the glass wall behind her desk. It ran the breadth of the suite of offices on the 17th floor of one of Cincinnati's tallest buildings. "Ain't nothing left but prom and graduation. Just haveta' figure who I'm taking."

"So that's it, you attend school for the girls and basketball?"

"I go to learn, to get an education. But besides my academics, I learn about other things," he grinned. "We still could take that ride, you know. The attorneys won't mind, since you work for me, anyhow."

"I know who I work for, Jonathan . . . "

"Me."

". . . this is my break time . . . "

"Me. You work for me." Posing, he shot a jumper toward the ceiling.

"Jonathan, I have no desire to ride in your expensive new toy. I hope you seriously contemplate your future. You're going to be a famous young man."

"Gonna be?" He cocked his head and shot another jumper.

"And I hope you can handle it. Now I must return to my work. If I want a career, I have to pass the exam. I don't possess basketball prowess, and I'm not the most famous young man in Ohio."

"You do that, 'cause I want you to be damn good when you reppin' me. Damn good. But you done messed up again, Counselor."

"How?"

"It's most famous in the 'nation,' not just in no Ohio," he laughed.

"I stand corrected. You probably are," she said, almost adding, "for the moment."

"Hey... how 'bout I pick you up after work? We still need to talk business, since you gone be my special assistant," he was backing up, grinning. Behind him, framed photos of sports stars graced the walls, as if he were backing into a hall of fame.

"Right," she said, hitting her textbook. "How about this, Jonathan, lunch? After your graduation and I pass the Bar. It'll be our dual celebration."

"Bet. I'ma be a millionaire by then."

O

Jonathan Jameer Gadsden, age 18, was labeled by sports reporters "the Cincy Rocket." Coach Sasser, who worked for the agents, finding and evaluating talent, called him *Johnny-Fly*, or *J-Fly*, because he skied so high. *The best damn big man I ever seen at his age.* A big-boned, Kentuckian, Coach Sass, as Jonathan called him, reminded Eden of the Johnny Carson sidekick from TV, only taller.

Sasser would chuckle, "That's what I love about these inner-city ball players. The best ones, they got that in-bred hunger, like racehorses, thoroughbreds. I can spot it by the way one of 'em walks in a gym. Don't

have to see 'em play, just watch their gait, the way they lope along like they in control of it all, 'cause they harbor a hunger that stays. I seen that hunger in J-Fly, and when I spot it in a player, I know he's a bonafide racehorse."

Racehorse. The first time Eden heard it applied to Jonathan, she thought of the stereotypes they'd discussed in black lit and considered resigning. But she needed this job. Furthermore, she knew what Sasser meant, because *she'd* entered law school hungry. She wasn't supposed to be in law school, a 24-year-old, divorced, working class white girl with a six-year-old son.

Seeing Benjy's photos on her desk, some asked, "Is that your little brother?"

And the hunger in her increased. Like the hunger following her divorce from her ex, the asshole. Or the hunger that prompted her to leave Xenia, her safety net of family and friends and move to Cincinnati for law school. The hunger of proving them wrong, her naysayers, her ex, and anyone else. The hunger of holding onto this job, $400.00 a week while learning the business of sports agency and caring for her son.

○

"Did the kid even attempt to flee?" Rudolph took off his glasses, gesturing with his hands.

"Rudy, why would he? He was driving a damn $80,000 SUV. Besides, J-Fly was on TV more than the freakin' governor. How could that cop *not* recognize him?"

"The officer said he was frightened and thought this big black kid was reaching for a weapon in his vehicle."

"A basketball. The kid was going in his truck for a damned ball," Cassinelli said, staring out the window behind Eden, at the bridges linking Ohio and Kentucky. "Fly's friend Monk-man said he was retrieving his basketball and news clippings to verify his identity."

"A ball. What the hell did the cop think he was gonna do? Cross him over to death?" Sasser shook his head.

"How's that statement coming, Eden?" Cassinelli asked, turning toward her. Three pairs of eyes stared her way. "You know the press conference is in two hours," Cassinelli added, his voice fluttering like when he'd called her last Saturday, 4:00 a.m., with the news.

"Eden, it's Mr. Cass. Eden, the kid is dead. Johnny's dead. Eden, J-Fly's been shot by a cop. He's dead. Dead."

"What? What are you talking about? Jonathan? Our Jonathan? Oh, no. Oh, no. Oh no . . ." She dropped the phone and ran to Benjy's room. Once there, she threw back the red blanket to make sure her child was there, buried safely.

"Benjamin, Benjy, Benjy," sitting on his bed, she stroked the covers. "Benjy, oh Benjy." She rubbed as though he were a magic lamp. "Benjy, oh, Benjy. Benjy."

"Huh, mommy, huh?" he stirred.

"Benjy, oh, my God. Benjy. Oh my God. Oh my God. No. No. No. No."

"Huh, mommy? What's wrong, Mommy?"

"Get up. Sleep next to mommy tonight. Oh my God. Oh no. Oh no."

"What is it Mommy?" he asked, rubbing sleepy eyes.

"Oh, Benjamin. Mommy's sorry to have awakened you, but something terrible's happened."

She thought of Jonathan's mother, Florence. His little sister Jamela and brother, Jafari, ages 13 and 15. The lawyers, the agency; she'd left Cassinelli hanging on the line. But she couldn't break the news to Benjy, and she couldn't stand up; so she climbed in bed beside him, pulling him close. Holding him tightly, she rocked him back to sleep. 'Til morning's light, Benjamin slept between her shoulders while she stared at the white walls of his room, plastered with Jonathan's basketball clippings and posters of athletes, mainly black ones, flying high, running fast.

○

From a park in Covington, KY, they faced the skyline of Cincinnati, the ballparks, the building where she worked. They ate lunch, burgers and fries, in her minivan. She'd refused to ride in Jonathan's monstrous SUV. Big, black, and with spinner wheels that cost 10 grand, it was an early high school graduation gift from his mom, although she worked as a cashier at a local store, financed by a seemingly unlimited line of credit from the agents. His high school graduation was in a week, the prom the day before. Her Bar Exam in two weeks, so this was the best time to fit in lunch. Jonathan was in demand: playing in various high school all-star games; seated in the front row at pro games in New York, Hot 'Lanta, L.A.; flying across the country; a celebrity, a star, part of the agency's marketing of him before the pro draft.

"Eden, how come you got books everywhere you go, all over this car and stuff?" He smiled, gesturing incredulity with big, outstretched hands.

"Same reason you carry a basketball everywhere."

"Aight," he said, staring at the books on the floor and seats of her old van and then out the windshield, at the bridge to Ohio, supporting a stream of cars. "Eden, I'ma have to go to summer school. Messed up in Language Arts. But I can still walk next week with my class, you know?"

"Jonathan, how'd you let that happen? I know how bright you are."

"I'on know," he shrugged. "Summer school's just four weeks. I just couldn't get into Shakespeare and 'nem."

"Why didn't you ask for help? I would've helped you. I was an English major in college."

"I remember. Just been too much been goin' on. First it was basketball season. Then, All-Star games. Now, I got interviews and appearances. Can't do all that stuff and book too," he shook his head. "But you wanna know something? One while, I used ta like school, especially Black History and that."

"My favorite class in college was Black Lit. I loved reading black writers, like Harriet Jacobs' slave narrative or Hurston and Baldwin. . . So now you have to attend summer school."

"E, I'ma be fine. Still goin' lottery pick in the draft. Hey," he said, reaching down for a book on the floor. "Since you done read all them black books and black history, tell me something, 'kay?"

"What, Jonathan? Why a white girl loves reading black literature?"

"Naw. Not that, I know you cool. You ever wonder how they did it, the slaves? How they got across the mountains and river to freedom?" he was turning the textbook over in his hands as she'd seen him do with a basketball, before a foul shot.

"Yes, I did. Especially after I read *Beloved*, by Toni Morrison.

"I saw the movie," he said.

"I brought Benjy here last fall, and we talked about the Underground Railroad and runaway slaves," she said, remembering. "I felt I needed to do that before he started school."

"I heard that. Never do know when they might be discussing slavery and that in kindergarten," he shook his head. "Benjy-Ben's gone be a bad little boy. I'ma teach him to hoop, you gone keep him straight with the books. That little boy's gone be bad. Bad," he laughed.

"He's always asking me to bring him by the office again so he can 'play with Jonathan.' When I pick him up from the daycare, the first thing he asks is, 'Did you see Jonathan today?' 'What's Jonathan wearing?' 'Is

Jonathan on TV tonight?' You have captured a little boy's heart, you know."

He flicked the book at the windshield as though shooting. "Benjy-Ben's my boy. I'ma get y'all season passes, so he can see me play whenever y'all want."

"He'll like that. But you don't know where you'll be playing. It could be anywhere in the country."

"No prob. You gone be on my payroll, my assistant, 'member?" He held his pose, his shot, as though his jumper was good and the game was won.

"Right, Jonathan," she said, stifling the objection in her throat.

"Hey Eden?"

"Yes, Jonathan?"

"Do any of 'nem books ever talk about how it was, gettin' free, crossin' that river?" he was staring at the book in his hands, or perhaps past it, at the river and bridges and sky.

Sighing, she stared at him; then, her eyes followed his. "According to what I studied, it wasn't just hard to escape, but there was an ongoing psychological struggle after the slaves escaped."

"So the struggle continues, huh?"

"Yes," she said. "I guess it does."

O

She was finishing her typing of the agency's statement.

"We at C&R Associates deeply regret the accidental shooting of our client, Jonathan Jameer Gadsden . . . We considered it an honor and privilege to represent such a talented young man with as much unlimited potential as Johnny . . ."

She stopped . . . because it wasn't *accidental*, anymore than that bridge across the river, or the slaves . . . She stared at them standing there, grown white guys in thousand dollar suits, deciding what they were going to do about the *accidental* death of an 18-year-old black boy who would've been worth millions to them.

What was *she* going to do? How many others had died like Johnny in *this* city? 15, 16, black males slain, by cops, in the past few years? How many in other cities, across the nation? Last night, unable to sleep, she'd gotten on the Net and read about other, similar deaths:

There was that other kid in Cincinnati, T. Thomas, age 19, unarmed, wanted for traffic violations and misdemeanors, shot and killed.

There was M. Hudspeth, in Shreveport, age 25, fatally shot by officers who mistook his cell phone for a gun.

There was P. Childs, a developmentaly disabled 15-year-old boy in Denver, who answered his door holding a knife, simply holding it, and was, like the others, shot and killed. According to witnesses, he didn't understand the officer's command to put down the knife. The officer standing next to the one who fired the weapon held a non-lethal Taser, but that wasn't fired.

After each slaying, there had been protests, marches, boycotts. And here, a brief riot. Maybe a lawsuit or settlement would follow. Then, nothing. Another dead manchild in the promised land. Some of the cases were still in court.

O

Benjy watched Mommy on TV. Jill, his baby sitter, watched too, eating popcorn like at a game. Mommy looked sad standing beside Jonathan's mom, sister, brother and the attorneys. They talked to reporters and answered questions.

"Mommy, I miss Jonathan," he said as they knelt to pray.

"I know."

"He was my friend."

"I know. He was our friend, Benjamin," she said, staring at J-Fly's poster on his wall. Benjy could look straight at it when he was in bed.

"Remember when he came over, Mommy?"

"I remember."

"After we played basketball, remember he bought burgers and we watched *Animal Planet?*

"I remember," she said, as she stared at Benjy's other posters: Jordan and other jocks.

"Then, 'member how we caught fire flies that night?"

"I remember. Benjamin, you have to say your prayers so I can tuck you in. Your mommy's had a long day."

"He jumped up and caught 'em. Jonathan snatched fire flies right out the sky."

"Yes, he did," she said, placing her arm around him.

She stared at the signed poster of Jonathan dunking a basketball, a blow-up of a magazine cover. She wanted to rip it down, but Benjy would cry.

Finally, he'd drifted off to sleep, after asking, "Why did the fireflies die, Mommy?"

"Maybe the holes in the jar weren't big enough."

"We made 'em big. Jonathan did."

"I know."

"I miss him, Mommy," he placed his head on her lap.

She stroked his head 'til he slumbered. She wanted them down, the posters on his walls of athletes in their glory. Little kids like Benjy adored and worshipped them. The world worshipped them. No, not worshipped—marketed, commodified, like slaves on a block, but the chains were platinum, gold. No, not slaves, messiahs—young black messiahs, each one a promised land of riches.

O

Mommy held his hand so tight it hurt. It was crowded outside the big, grey church. In the street, so many cars and trucks that they couldn't move, and police officers and TV people were everywhere. Across from the church, people were carrying signs. Some of them, Benjy could read: "Cops Kill Black Men."

She held his hand and pushed against people as they climbed the steps. She was whispering something. The music coming from inside the church was Tupac Shakur and reminded him of when he rode in Jonathan's truck.

"Benny-Ben, I be blasting little man. Blastin'." Flowers and large posters of Jonathan were all around the church. The church smelled like a flower garden. On the posters, Jonathan looked alive, jumping, dunking, shooting. The church was crowded. Mr. Cassinelli waved for Mommy and him to come up front, but she shook her head no and led him to the seats in back. Then, a movie screen slid down and a video began.

"J-Fly steals the ball, dribbles downcourt, takes off at the foul line and tomahawk-dunks the rock.

"Did you see that? A 180 degree switch-the-ball from the left to the right, a windmill dunk! Isn't this kid fab?

"Jonathan J-Fly Gasden drives the length of the court, weaving through defenders like a halfback.

"He's got all the skills. One through three in the upcoming draft. Some scouts say as low as five, but he'll be gone by then . . . "

Some people stood and clapped. Mommy squeezed his hand tighter, and he knew she wouldn't let go.

A choir of kids was singing, beating drums and tambourines. He couldn't hear all of the words. The music was too loud. Jonathan's little

sis, Jamella, was singing, too. She was pretty. He knew her name from the funeral program, and because Jonathan had talked about his sister and brother. People got up and danced. They cheered, waving at the ceiling, like at one of Jonathan's games, and he was putting on a show. The choir sang, *Goin' up Yonder*, and *He's my Rock*, until the church was hot and sweaty and his eyes burned. Mommy's did too, or she was sweating, because her face was so wet he wanted to wipe it.

The tall lady preacher had long, thick hair that looked like ropes you could swing on. She wore a purple and gold robe, like a queen.

She said, "Even the youths shall faint and be weary, and the young men shall fall."

He didn't know all the words, but knew she was talking about Jonathan. Reaching in his pocket for the peppermint candy, he unwrapped it with one hand, using his fingers. He wanted to offer Mommy a piece. The reverend lady preached about the *Lord and . . . eagle's wings* while walking around the church. The church organ screeched and wailed. The reverend lady screamed, repeating her words over and over, and some people rose up and shouted back. When she spoke, her hair shook, like weeping willow branches in a storm.

"Mommy, what are we gonna put in the casket?" he whispered. She didn't answer, but looked sad, like when she was on TV. "Mommy, Mommy?"

"What Benjy?" he could tell she was upset.

"Nothing," he said, finding a piece of candy in his suit pocket with his hand.

When they got to the casket, she was whispering, "No, this shouldn't be. This shouldn't be."

She touched Jonathan's chest for a second and prayed something, like when she tucked him in bed. Inside the casket, lying beside Jonathan's body, were a tiny basketball, a white rose and a folded basketball jersey from the team.

Benjy dropped his candy in the casket, careful that his hand didn't touch anything. "Bye, Jonathan. Bye."

She wondered why Benjy had done it. Kids. Maybe he would need counseling. But it was good he was spending time with Jafari. They were playing basketball on a goal at the end of the church parking lot.

"Come join us," Florence said, instructing Coach Sass to make room for Eden at the head table. The table of mourners at which she and Benjy ate had gone through the buffet line, served by smiling sisters and brothers

dispensing scoops of greens, sweet potatoes, macaroni and cheese, and baked beans. Those at the head table sat and were served all these along with golden fried chicken, corn bread and desserts. Eden was full. She followed Florence to the head table, though she'd enjoyed watching the attorneys squirm throughout the meal, as if Rev. Veronica Spikes was going to shout *hallelujah,* and start preaching again. Or perhaps they felt the plastic folding chairs would break if they breathed. They hadn't eaten much. Coach Sass, on the other hand, was on his third helpings. Sitting across from Florence, Eden sought solace in the older woman's eyes. Big, African eyes, like Jonathan's.

"Your baby's fine," Florence said, reading her mind. "Jafari won't let nothing happen to him."

"Yes, and Benjy won't let nothing happen to Jafari," Eden smiled at her own ungrammatical response. Florence did not smile.

"Jonathan admired you, you know."

"He was my friend, my buddy, almost like a little brother."

"Said he could talk to you, that you was real. Are you?"

"I hope so. We talked a lot. He came in every day." She almost added, "carrying new trinkets each time."

"Well, the agency's gonna keep representing us, you know."

"Yes, I know, a pending lawsuit."

"Yes, but right now, they're going to start representing Jafari."

"Jafari?" Eden said, peering down the table at the attorneys, who were watching them.

"They're taking him on as a client, just like Jonathan."

"So soon? How can you? . . ."

"How can I what?" Florence interrupted. "Come here," she said, rising and striding toward a basement window. Eden followed. Once there, they saw her soaring baby boy leap through the air to the goal, his black tie loosened, streaming behind him like a banner. "According to Coach Sass, Jafari is ranked in the top five in the nation for a fifteen year old." Florence's expression was steel. "Top five," she repeated. "He can write his own ticket. I got agents all over the country vying for him."

"Jafari's good alright," Eden said. "Just like Jonathan," she added, hoping Florence caught it.

"Both of my boys can really play that ball," Florence said, staring out the window.

"No. Both of them cannot. Jonathan is dead. And we killed him. All of us. How can you do this?"

"Do what?"

"Trust any of it?" Eden recalled the time Jonathan had given Benjy basketball lessons, and a crowd had gathered at the suburban, elementary school court, to watch and take photos.

"Wait just a minute, Miss. My son is dead. Gone. And one of my surviving babies has that dream too. Now, I don't know who you think killed my baby, but I know it was some white racists, and they are gonna pay. I can't bring my boy back, but I can make sure we get paid. I can make sure somebody pays for his death. And those white men over there are gone help me. Do you understand?"

She shook her head, and the beads in her braids clicked, bouncing against each other. "I said, do you understand?"

"Yes, I understand," Eden said, forcing a smile, thinking of runaways, peppermint candy, and fireflies. On the drive from the cemetery back to the church, Benjy had asked, "Are you mad at me, Mommy?"

"Why would I be mad?"

"Because I put my candy in Jonathan's casket. I would have put my firefly jar, but I forgot to bring it."

"No, I'm not mad."

"No, you don't understand." Florence's words grabbed Eden, pulling her back to the present. "You can't begin to understand. Nobody can. When I rise up in the morning, I think, 'When is my baby coming home?' Maybe he's just on a road trip with his team or traveling with Coach and them, but he's gone, Missy Miss. Gone. Do you understand? My boy's gone."

"Yes . . . No." Eden shook her head. "I'm sorry. You're right. No, I don't understand."

Then, she turned; they turned, toward the sounds outside: their sons sweating up their dress clothes, caught in the thrill of Jafari, shouting like a warrior he as leaped up and slammed the ball hard through the goal, and Benjy, laughing, running to retrieve it for him. "I don't understand any of it," she whispered, wondering what *she* would have placed in the casket. "But I can't work for the agents anymore. I just can't. And we must go. Bar exam's this week."

"Well, you gotta work for somebody," Florence said, touching Eden's shoulder, resting her hand there. "And my kid trusted *you*. Besides, we both got kids to raise. We both got sons."

"Yes, you're right," Eden said, moving away from Florence's touch, turning to the agents as she went toward the door. "But I know *they're* glad you have one more."

Notes:

19-year-old Timothy Thomas, unarmed, was shot and killed by a policeman in Cincinnati, Ohio, April 7, 2001.

25-year-old Marquise Hudspeth, whose cellular phone was mistaken for a pistol, was shot and killed by police in Shreveport, Louisiana, March 15, 2003.

15-year-old Paul Childs, a special-needs child who suffered from both mental retardation and epilepsy, was shot and killed in Denver, Colorado, July 5, 2003.

There are these cases, and others, of young black men (like 23-year-old Sean Bell, unarmed, shot and killed by New York City Police on his wedding day, November 25, 2006) who have died in needless police shootings.

Homeless M.F.

Homeless M.F.

My sign says "Work for money or food."

"I'll give you sex," she says, smiling, black like me.

I get in her car: big BMW 735, jet black, like the night. I want to steal the MF. I keep my sign close to me, in front of my holely, dirty clothes.

"Put down that piece of cardboard," she orders, sounding like a prison guard or one of the people who runs the shelter where I go for a bed and food.

"My clothes aren't clean."

"I didn't pick you up for your clothes or your sign." She floors the pedal with a black suede, high-heeled pump. She's taking the skyway, north, toward the Falls and Canada. The black leather seat cradles me, and I want to go to sleep. It's been years since I've been in anything this soft.

"Wake up," she says, knocking the sign out of my grasp and to the floor.

I want to say, *Bitch, what's your problem*, but don't. I want to retrieve my sign, but don't. Instead, I pretend there's an imaginary tunnel in the sky. I see her out the corner of my eye. I can't close my eyes, but I want to. Her left hand and wrist sparkle with diamonds and gold as she holds the steering wheel and the speedometer rises: 70 mph. Her right hand, which has more money on it, grips the stick shift. We're moving into the tunnel. She's staring at my sign, like she dares me to touch it. I don't play dares. Since I was released, my sign has been my way of *getting' over*, a scam I picked up from Rodney. The least I get from it is food; sometimes clothes, anything I can sell, or some chump change. When I'm picked up by some lame who *pays* me first, probably thinking that a *homeless m.f.* like me needs to eat *before* doing their bidding, I walk. Eat their food, take what I can, and split. When I work, I also steal, things which won't be missed right away and won't cause them to go to the cops.

"I'm hungry," I say, thinking of how I'd been about to call it a night when she'd stopped.

"I'll satiate your hunger."

"What?"

She takes the car higher: 80 mph. "The word 'satiate' means to . . ."

"I know what it means," I interrupt her. I hate black people like her, want to smack her across her fine-ass face with my sign.

"What, then?" She's reflected in the black windshield. She's not that old, probably fine in her day, but not bad now, 'pecially with her money.

"You're not my teacher." I don't tell her about how I study the dictionary, like Malcolm.

"I could be, in anything you want." She turns on the stereo and pushes the car past 90. Never been in a car like this, want to drive it. Want to drive her, sex. Never done an older babe.

Toni Braxton, one of those sisters who can blow like Sunday morning, is singing *Breathe Again*. It's all around me, like this bitch's perfume.

So I dare her. "You should be scared. I'm a homeless m.f. with a record." She takes the car to a hundred. Never been on a plane, but if I could close my eyes, I'd be flyin'. Been this fast once before. She ain't backing down, but neither am I.

"I was in 'cause I wasted somebody. Tisha, my baby sister, was shot in a drive-by. One night, she was sitting on the porch, watchin' me wash my ride, a black '83 Mustang. We'd been just jokin' and laughin'. Tish could sing, like this sister, and she was singin' when it happened. *A House is Not a Home*, playin' with it, like Luther, you know? Then, *bam, bam, bam*, shots, lights, my baby sister's blood, on the porch, on my ride, on me. She made it to me, died in my arms. I put her down on that hard-ass porch. I had to. I put her down. Got in my ride and chased them m.f.'s for I don't know how long. I was hauling ass, like in the movies. Somethin' just came over me, seeing Tisha down on that porch, bleeding, when minutes before she'd been singing: Luther and Minnie Riperton. You might not remember Minnie, but Tish used ta love her, could reach any note Minnie could. That was five years ago. They was low-life drug dealers, and it was my first offense, so I here I am."

"Yes, here you are." Her hand strokes my thigh. I'm gettin' hard. I try to focus on my scam: food, money. Try to focus on why I been goin' out, to get some money to get a place. Stayin' at the Homeless Shelter near downtown, on Swan. Sometimes there ain't enough beds or food, or somebody gets knifed . . . almost as bad as the joint . . . was released five weeks ago and don't intend to go back.

"Yeah," I say, repeating her repeating me, "here I am." I don't want this babe. She's not that old, maybe 30 or 35, tops, and I ain't been with a woman in *so* long, but this don't seem logical, so I try to use my words to stop her hands, cause my hands sure the hell ain't gonna. "It was in all the papers," I say, wanting to scream, 'cause I'm telling my story again, for, as momma would say, the umpteenth time.

"I know," she says.

I want to scream, 'cause this babe is stroking my jones to hardness and her perfume is strong, and this ride is one bad piece of blackness. I want to scream, 'cause this white-acting babe has scared me like a mafuh. Feel I got to scream.

"M.F.'s shot at the wrong house," I say. "You know, they played it up big in the news. I was on the front page a couple of times: when they arrested me, and when they convicted me. Even a couple of t.v. stations wanted to interview me, but all I wanted was to be left alone. Nothing they could do would bring back my sister."

She says something like "I know" again, but I don't really hear her, 'cause I want to shut up, know I'm rambling, know I ain't talked like this since before Tisha's death. During the trial I spoke to momma and my attorney, a sharp dressing babe like this one, but white, who thought all bruhs was low-life, potential killers and didn't care who I killed or why.

Some in the community said I was a hero and should get off "scott-free" 'cause of what had happened to Tish and it'd been a drug dealer and I'd been clean. Clean. I'd carried a gun 'cause you had to at certain high schools in Buffalo, 'pecially if you weren't big or loud or in a gang. I'd been clean—no record—not like now.

But I'd spent my "senior prom night" in Attica State Prison. And had adopted silence and a *kill me if you can look* in order to keep the m.f. hounds off my *young, tender behind*.

Toni B is singing, *Love Should've Brought You Home Last Night*. My hand strokes the honey's arm as her hand touches my stomach, thighs, and then fishes down into my pants. Her fishing hand finds its catch, and the car hits 110.

"I know what you need," she says, and her voice is cool and dry, like her hand. I want to close my eyes and moan, hum, like the engine, but I talk.

"Five m.f. years. Momma died after two. She was all I had left. I finished school inside. Got into shape, stayed on good behavior. Even got an Associates, but who gon hire me? A con? I never say 'ex,' cause once you a con, that's it. It's like that AA thing. Once an alcoholic, always. Don't care what you do after that, it's over, 'specially if you're black." Her hand is warm, sweaty now, like me.

"Pull over."

"Why? We're almost there, baby," she smiles, emphasizing the last word.

"What about food?" I don't know where we are, somewhere on the way to Canada, between Buffalo and Niagara Falls.

"I want to eat, too," she says, feeling my jones.

"Where we goin'? You're good with your hands and all, baby, but I can do that myself." I grab her wrist and pull her hand out of my pants like I'd seen a con pull a knife out of a man. I throw it back at her. "I need food and money. And if you want me to *work* for you, you gone haveta feed me."

She grabs her arm like I've hurt it. Her face becomes stone. I'm glad. "Okay, let's stop now." She puts on the brakes, hard, like when I caught up to my sister's killers at a light and hit them m.f.'s with everything I had. She turns off the CD.

I stare out the window as the car leaves the highway. "Satiate means to satisfy," I say. "Remember, said I want to eat."

"There's food in the trunk." She shifts with the hand which was touching me and wheels the ride into a rest stop, near Lake Erie. She points at a little building. No other cars here. "We can eat here, they've got pop machines inside." She opens a console behind the stick shift, showing a few bills and some change. "Here's money for pop." I want to take it and run. I want to eat the food I came out for. Want to screw this woman. Want to satiate the hunger I've felt since I lost Tish, my baby sis, my ace. She gets out the car, taking her purse and keys. I stare at her legs, body, mink coat, jewelry. And follow. Looking back, she smiles and locks the ride with a remote. I was in a dream inside that car, but this cold-ass night is reality. The hawk, coming down from Canada, blowing her, blowing through me, is reality. She reaches the building and pulls a gun out of her mink coat. "Satiate means to satisfy fully, Terrence."

I stop. And try to recall her, to sprint back through five years. She says something like, "Willie Parker, the man you killed, was my man. I didn't attend the trial, but I was attentive to your life, 'cause what you did to me and mine, I'm going to do to you," but I hear red-neck prison guards spitting out "nigger." She points her piece at me, but I see some big m.f. in the joint tryin' to punk me. She's standin' there, rich and fine and havin' scammed me when I was tryin' to scam her. But I see Tisha.

I pull out my knife and throw it, with the practice of time in the joint. I know where it's gone hit, cause Tisha is still singin' to me, playin' with her voice, holding her note. My blade hits where I aimed it, the arm that holds the gun. She falls, dropping it, and it fires into the night. Tisha is still singing as I ease the knife from her flesh, holding a note forever, a high note, up there like Minnie or Denise Williams or somebody. Blood saturates her black silk blouse. I rip it, revealing her black bra and smooth brown cleavage. She's too hurt to do anything but look at me in tears as I use what I ripped to help make a tourniquet. I find her gun and heave it into the dark. I pour out her purse: bills, cosmetics, credit cards, jewelry, and keys; they sparkle on the grass like Christmas lights. I take the keys and unlock her car, using the remote. Easing into the driver's seat, I start the m.f. It purrs, hums. I lock myself in. Turn on everything, the lights, stereo, heated seats. I can sleep in here. "Live in this m.f.," I say to myself. In the headlights, I see her in front of me, in my imaginary tunnel. I can run her over. Can take this m.f. and go to Canada or anywhere.

I turn off the sounds, listen to the engine.

And I hear Tisha. My sis is still singin', holding that note, like in church, when she did it 'til they got happy, and I did, too, without showin' it. I cut off the engine and take the chump change she was gone give me to get sodas. I leave my sign on the floor of the car and get out. I shoot the sister's keys at the building, like b-ball on the prison yard; they bounce off, not far from her. Bucket. I walk away on the grass between the lake and the highway, not looking behind me for coming cars, not wanting to hitch back to Buffalo.

"This gone take awhile," I think, holding myself against the cold air and seeing, through my tears and the night, Tisha's face, smiling, as she finishes her song.

Junior Aint

Junior Aint

I took 'em from under the tree and brought 'em into my room 'cause I'm tired of Skipper and Jody coming over and breaking 'em. Every Christmas, it's the same old thing, my cousins come over to our house, play with my toys and break one of 'em. It's like Jody does it on purpose. I hate having 'em visit on Christmas. Yeah, I know, we go over to their house later on in the day, like Mom says, *It's the family Christmas ritual. The way we stay close, Junior.*

Well, I started my own ritual. First I was surprised mom didn't say much when I took my toys upstairs. "Cynthia, I guess maybe your baby brother's growing up. Look at him, picking up all the wrapping paper and carrying his toys to his room."

"Yeah, right, mom." Cynthee kept right on spying out the front room window, focusing her new telescope.

"Honey, don't you want your cousins to see your new toys?"

"Mommy, they can see em," I said, runnin' up the stairs with my trucks and remote control 'Vette in my arms.

I spit on 'em. Let 'em play with 'em now. You can't even see the spit, I brushed it on so good. Been workin' on my plan since last week, after Uncle Deon came over and dropped off some food. That's what I don't understand, here they got more money than us and a big house 'n all, and two, no, three cars; well, a truck and two cars, and my cousins gotta come over here and break my toys? Not this year.

So I started spittin' in my jar right after Uncle Deon left; really, right after I finished chompin' down the Kentucky Fried he left for us. The thing is to spread it on nice and thin, so it makes 'em shine better, makes 'em look newer. When they come, I'm gone say, *Y'all, my toys is put up already.* But I know Jody, she ain't gone take no for an answer; she's nosey like that, like Aunt Patty, and Uncle De' too. Half the time coming over just to see what we doin', or, like mom say, *how we doin'*, like we need they help. We don't, and I'm gone show 'em we don't.

"So, Junior, you get any more toys for Christmas?"

"Naw," I say, cause I really don't wanna' do it, 'cause I hid my best toy, my remote control 'Vette, next to my spit jar in the closet, so they can't even see it. I don't wanna do it, not even to nosey ole' Jody. "Besides," I say, "my name ain't Junior. It's Willam."

"It's whatever I say it is, Junior. You're right, your name can't be Junior anyway, 'less you got a senior."

Jody's just wheeling my dump truck back and forth, back and forth, cross the rug. Skipper's playin' on my Nintendo, and he not saying nothin', 'cause he don't like to pick sides, and he knows how me and Jody always go at it. Sometimes, when we alone, he says it's 'cause she really likes me, think I'm her best baby cousin, but I don't believe him. I don't like her at all.

"It's whatever I say it is, boy," Jody says. "I think I'ma start calling you Willie, 'cause you ain't no Junior anyway, can't be, without a . . ."

Then, she just stops, like she know I know where she goin', so she don't even need to go there.

"Willie, mind if I take a nap on your bed? I'm getting bored, with only these toys. When are you-all coming over to our house? We got a new Sega Genesis, and a whole lotta games, and . . . oops, I'm sorry, I didn't mean to say I don't like your toys and all, it's just that Nintendo is wack," she says, stretching out on my bed.

"I got another toy."

"You do?"

"Yeah, I almost forgot."

"How can you forget a toy you just got today? Boy, you fibbin'. You just didn't want me playin' with your toys."

"Naw, that ain't it, tell her, Skip," I say to Skipper, who's into that Nintendo game like he's Scottie Pippen. He's playin' NBA Live, one of my old games. He always plays it when he comes over, thinks he can hoop.

"My name is Bennett, and I ain't in it," Skip says, and don't even look at me or her. He's kickin' the game's butt, as usual.

"Okay, Jody, you got me," I say, lookin' at myself in the mirror above the dresser. I'm getting' kinda tall, gone be big, like my daddy, Mom's always sayin'. "I'ma go get my other toy, the one I been savin' for you. You just stay right there and rest; I'll put it together real quick, okay?"

"Okay," she say. She got her eyes closed, like she gone take a nap on my bed and ain't nothin' I can do 'bout it. I'm pouring my spit on my 'Vette, like it's somebody being baptized in church. I'm spreading it all over, so it's nice and wet and sticky. Then I spit some more on my car, 'cause there ain't enough on there already. I'm cryin' and wipin' my tears and getting' spit on my face and tears on my 'Vette when I spread the spit some more.

I'm standin' up in this dark closet, getting' ready to go out. Gotta do this, 'cause I do have a daddy. 'Cause I'm tired of Jody and everybody tellin' me I don't, tellin' us we poor; so I'ma show her, show her good. My face is wet, but I don't care. Holding my 'Vette close so it don't fall, I open the door. My TV and Nintendo's on, but ain't nobody playin', Bulls

Another Continent

"What are you waiting for?"

"I don't know. No, the truth is I don't want to be a two-time loser."

"You're not; you're my dream woman." Behind her, the Potomac River shone in the moonlight, and I wished it was warm enough to eat outside.

"Yeah, well, Kenny was my dream man," Val spoke, staring, her brown eyes big, bold. "It's strange, all this talk about there not being enough professional black men in D.C., because I've had my share and then some. Here I was, with a kid and a wrecked marriage, and then along comes Prince Charming with a Benz and a good job with the government."

"Can't forget that G.S. rating," I joked.

"Right," she said, giving me a smirk. "Kenny came along and helped me feel special again, like a woman again."

"So?" I said, hating the sound of his name.

"So I found out he's a dog, and I don't sleep with dogs, just nice guys like you. I love *you*," she said, emphasizing the last word, as though I hadn't heard it before.

"Val, I don't want to just sleep with you. I want to wake up with you. Wait on you. Do whatever you expect from a man." The background music, a sista blowing hard, reaching hard, high notes, seemed to support me.

"Cain, you know I expect nothing from a man. Nothing, that's why I can stay with Kenny."

"Kenny the dog from whom you're separated, but it's really not a separation, because he comes home periodically."

"You know that's what he does."

"So then it's really no different than when you were together."

"I'll ignore that."

"I don't want you to. You're wasting your life, Val."

"It's my life." She stared at me and then at Joseph, our waiter. He was stationed close enough to hear every word. No one else was on this side of the restaurant, since it was only 7:00 p.m. and most of the Friday patrons came to party, not eat. They would arrive later.

She looked Joseph up and down: his nappy, uncombed hair; his round, African face, jet black and shiny. His crisp white shirt and black slacks, hands at his side, him standing there, as though he were a sentry, guarding us.

Then, as if summoned, Joseph approached our table. "Dr. C.," he said, looking at Val, but addressing me, "is everything alright? Would you like anything else?"

As he spoke, I remembered our initial meeting. He and two other Rwandan students stopped by my university office.

"The African Students United is hosting our annual Rwandan Youth Conference here this weekend. University policy dictates that at all times we must have faculty sponsors at the event. Will you help us, and be one of our faculty sponsors, sir?"

He told me his story: how he'd survived the slaughter in Rwanda. And I'd agreed to help, to be a sponsor perhaps as a way to assuage feelings of guilt.

"No, nothing, thank you," Val said, before I could respond.

"Water, Joseph," I said, smiling.

"Yes, Dr. C.," he said, turning away.

Whenever Rwanda is mentioned, I remember Joseph's story; I try to piece it together as best as I can. I try to remember his voice as we sat in my office that afternoon.

"We, my parents and I, were trying to escape the hunters, the slayers. We tried to drive to Kigali, so perhaps we could flee the country. We had friends outside who would help. My father was Tutsi and my mother, Hutu. To escape, my mother drove the car, while my father hid in the trunk. I sat in the back seat of the car. At some point, when we reached the city, we had to split up."

"Splitting up" meant that Joseph eventually made it safely to Tanzania, but he never saw his parents again. When he spoke, his eyes teared up.

"Dr., I just miss them." Saying this, he pulled out a photo of a smiling couple with a brown little boy that could have been taken in Cleveland, Atlanta or here in D.C.

When I attended the Rwandan Youth Confereence, they spoke in languages I didn't understand, so I just sat there, staring at the men and women and laughing at the hungry children, going back and forth past me to the tables of punch, cookies and chips at the rear of the room. Recently, I'd been reading about another massacre in the Motherland, another African genocide, this one in the Sudan, and seeing him always made me feel inadequate and guilty as though I should have done more. More, more.

More. Val and I worked at the university where I was a professor and she an Associate Dean and director of a college prep program for inner-city kids. During the summer, she hired high school teachers to instruct her kids and college profs as guest lecturers. As a new black prof., I'd been recommended to teach in her program. She'd asked me to lecture for her program, on *Black Rhetorical Traditions*.

"Like what?" I'd asked.

"Like your favorite pick-up lines, not that you have to use any."

I'd consented to lecturing in her program. I also consented to an urge to discover more about this woman. Thirty-nine, though she looked ten years younger. A sharp dresser. A man-killer. A flirt. Lots of fun. A sister with her head on straight. A sister who couldn't pick a good man. These and more were what I heard around campus concerning Val. From her, only one: "Sincere. I'm just looking for that one right relationship."

And I wanted to give it to her. At first, our meetings centered on work. My recent completion of the Ph.D. Her research, on Womanist theory in higher ed and mine, on black rhetoric and speech. I joked that she could hire me when she became a university president. She'd secured numerous grants for her summer program, which boasted a success rate of over 95%. She was working on book number three, while I was struggling with my first real manuscript. Around the time of Kenny's third or fourth extramarital affair, our "meetings" became dates. The first time we kissed was the weekend she issued Kenny an ultimatum, either shape up, or . . . So he'd negotiated a transfer out of D.C., to give them time and space.

But it was taking too much time, and she needed too much space, from me. They lived separate lives, but according to her, "If I divorce Kenny, I'll have no one." Evidently, I was no one.

"Hey, Cain, wake up," Valerie said, patting my face with her hand.

"I'm awake."

"Okay, then here it is again," she said, holding her wine glass but not sipping. "These things take time. I'm not asking you to wait. You can go your merry way."

"Val, even if I didn't love you, I wouldn't want you to stay with Kenny. It's wrong."

"No, Cain, we're wrong. I'm still married. Besides, I've been managing my life and Jimmy's by myself for years, so I think I know what I'm doing. Like I said, gallant knight, it's my life."

"Yeah, but what about mine?" I moved my knife to the middle of the small table, between our place settings. "I mean, what do we do, continue seeing each other or what? I'm tired of this professional relationship/ friendship crap." I positioned the salt shaker on one side of my knife, and the pepper shaker on the other.

"Well, that's what we have, hon. A professional relationship, a friendship and something else." Val gave a me smirk. "What part don't you want? Like I said, I'm not asking you to wait."

"What are you asking, then?" I picked up my fork and tapped on the table.

"Cain, I'm not asking you, or any man, for a damned thing." She slid the fork from my hand and placed it down. "That's why I'm not in a relationship."

"What do you call us?" I felt like pushing our table through the window, off the patio and into water, to show her I could make it float.

"I call us good friends; that's all. People who will always feel deeply for each other."

"When you say deep, I think of . . ."

"Stop. I'm still married, and what we shared once doesn't make us lovers. Besides, I'm trying to get closer to God."

"Me, too," I say. "But it was twice. And you're separated."

"Whatever," she said. "Still married, still alone, really." Then, she winked. "Besides, that quickie in my office doesn't count, 'cause now I know your real talents. Eat up, I have to leave in a bit, pick up my kid. Kenny's arriving in town later tonight, and we've got a lot to discuss."

"I'm not hungry. And you know you won't discuss anything. You'll continue to let that asshole keep you on a string, and . . ."

"And it's my business. Nobody else's. Now eat. You're in training, remember? Gonna give me ten more pounds of muscle by December. Order some dessert, love. My treat."

"I thought we were going to make some decisions."

"I have. We'll have a double celebration. My newest book contract and you finally finishing your manuscript." She rubbed my thigh under the table.

I moved my leg away from her touch. "Yeah, maybe by then we'll have made love three times."

"Whatever," she said, placing her hands on the table.

"Excuse me, Val," I said, scooting back my chair, rising from the table. "I'll be back in a sec."

"I know," she said, smiling.

I resented her smile, her sense of control. Valerie Shaw-Warren, Ph.D., seemed so in control, so supreme, with everything and everyone but that fool, her husband. Splashing my face with water, I gazed in the restroom mirror. I loved her, but so what? Our relationship couldn't progress, just like I couldn't step into this mirror. Or walk across the water with her to Africa.

I locked the door to the restroom. Reaching in my pockets, laid my wallet, keys and bills on the counter. Took off my watch and silver bracelet and laid them down, too. After pulling my shirt over my head, I stared at the mirror. Yeah, I loved her. Would try to walk on water, like Jesus, for her. But what could I give her? We both wanted to be closer to God. But who didn't? In this crazy mixed-up world, where what I'd discarded meant something, how could I help her? Help myself? Her marriage was a joke. And maybe I was, too.

What would Joseph say right now? He'd survived genocide. Hunters. Killing fields strewn with black bodies. Joseph later told me that one of the languages in which they spoke that afternoon was *Kinyarwanda*, a Bantu language. There were so many languages I did not speak. Like Val's. And I too had allowed Africa to perish. I too allowed it to continue suffering: murder and rape in Darfur, Sudan, the rampage of AIDS, disease, poverty. *You black Americans have it easy*, Joseph would say. Since meeting Joseph, I'd quizzed my student-friend numerous times. I'd read books, attended forums, watched documentaries on the killings in Rwanda. But I guess I was daydreaming when they occurred. *You black Americans don't care what happens in Africa*, Joseph would say. *You just want to wear African garb and imitate our dances. Dr. C., there are so many pressing problems back home.* My problem was, I needed to send her back home, to her husband. Or maybe I needed a new home. She was still with him. She hadn't really *left* him, and wouldn't, not until that ass had trashed her life like her first one, because of her belief about never wanting to doubt that *I gave my all*. Hell, I needed her all. Needed and wanted the language, the tongues, to convince her to trust me.

"I want you to make a decision, Val. Now." I stood over our table.

"My decision is no decision. Sit down, Cain."

But sitting would only lead to standing up again, to follow her around like a starving child craving food. It broke my heart to watch those documentaries on Africa, to see malnourished suffering black babies, flies lighting on their faces. I wanted to be able to whisk away the flies, enter TV-land and somehow save those babies. Once, I'd told Valerie my desire to adopt an African infant, perhaps one with AIDS. She'd laughed: *Cain, I've been raising a child, by myself. You haven't. And when I'm done with this one, I ain't raising no more. But we can give to the cause.*

"Cain, sit down." Her voice brought me back.

"I don't feel like sitting," I said, holding onto the chair.

"Then what do you feel like doing, dearheart?" *Dearheart* was her most tender pet name for me. Her mom had called her dad this through 40

years of marriage. They were both deceased, her mother most recently, just months before we met.

"Valerie, you know I can't do what I feel like doing." I said, gripping the chair, although I wanted to hold her, as though our lives depended on it. Wanted to wrap my arms around her, providing warmth like a blanket. Wanted to shelter her, like a tree or cave, so no one could harm her, find her. Instead, her hunters would find me; they would have to come through me.

Valerie smiled. "Just be patient, Cain. Eventually, we'll be able to, all the time," she said, thinking she could read my mind.

"I am patient," I said, releasing the chair.

"Good. Now please sit down," she said, the bright blackness of the window behind her displaying the sparkling Potomac.

"No, Val, I'm just gonna stand."

"Well, since you're standing, I'll join you," and she nodded at Joseph for the check. I stared as she rose and looked in her purse in order to pay. At 5'9", she was tall enough to model for two years with the Ebony Fashion Show. While on tour, she met and married a possessive fool who *forbade his woman from working,* and abused her. Thank goodness she eventually left. I stared at my Val, a tough, smart sister who was *scared of a second marriage* but did it anyway, for romance or hope or her then-infant son, to a man who didn't smother her, but instead gave her the space of America, so he could possess the expanse of Africa. Some brothers—they don't realize what they have. As studied her, I saw Black-Sister-Woman strength: I recalled when I first knew I loved her. I was day-dreaming out of my office window when I spied her walking across campus, toward another building. I grabbed my keys.

"Not bad, Dr. C," she said after I caught up with her, and she handed my manuscript to me. I'd asked her to critique it. I hadn't known how long it would take her to finish reading it. She wore African garb that day, bright oranges and gold that complimented her bronze skin and long auburn locs. As we walked, I was proud to be close to her. She shone.

"Ya think?"

"Yeah, I think you got something there, Doc."

"I think I do too," I said.

Some brothas—they don't realize what they have. I did, and as she handed the money to Joseph, I stared at Valerie, as though the sax was reciting her story, how she worked her way from a secretary's job, earning three degrees, while raising Jimmy and caring for sick, aging parents who eventually died.

"Val, you're an African queen, you know that?" I said, smiling.

"Gallant knight, that's an old, tired line."

"I know, Dr. Val." Leaning over, I closed my eyes and kissed her. "I know." Opening them, I looked at Joseph. "You're a queen, but I can't reign with you." Then I looked away, at neither him nor her, but out the window, at water, leading to an ocean, another continent.

It Falls Between

It Falls Between

Two men: one, black; one, white.

Black:

Funky, cuz I ain't washed up in days. Like momma used to say, "so funky you can smell yourself, so you know somebody else can smell it." Still, I gotta be out here, gotta make some money. Iris is like, "Harry, you can't make no money wipin car windows. Gettin up at 6 a.m. Ain't nobody out at that time. You crazy." But I ain't crazy. Just tryin to hustle, make some ends. Like momma used to say, "anything is better than stealin'."

White:
Here I am, driving around these filthy streets. Every Saturday, the same ritual, because I must. It has been a year, and the cops have turned up nothing. All they know is a black man murdered our daughter. They're useless. The cops, because it shouldn't take a year to find one murdering, useless punk; the niggers, because . . . No, like I said before I left this morning, "Louise, as far as I'm concerned, there's only one nigger in the whole damned world, the one who murdered Rebecca. Her murderer, and I'm going to find him and get justice." Becca would be 23 this week. Louise would be getting on with her life, instead of visiting the grave on Sundays.

Last night, I say, "Iris, I can make some money on that there corner." And she like, "Harry, you might as well just go get you a cup and some pencils. Why don't you get a real job? Don't come back here 'til you bringing something in to help out." But she don't understand. You can't just get a job like that in Buffalo, not with no record, anyhow.

Louise said, "At least take that murder sign off Becca's truck. It appears you're mad at the world." I am. Especially this morning . . . a year. A year. Look at the black on the corner. Staring at me as I pass. He could be the one.

Gone show Iris my "sorry ass" can get a job, even if I got to make up one. This gone be a good day. Like momma used to say, "every day you got life a good day." This bout the second time that white truck been round the block. Don't look like no cop car. Wonder what he want? "Window wash!" Maybe he's wondering what I'm doin' out here. "Window wash!"

Louise said, "Don't go into the ghetto looking for Becca's killer, all you'll find is trouble." Well, I may have found it. What's he shouting at me?

Rodney say, "Harry, man, the way the brothas do it in Philly and New York is they just run up to stopped cars, start wipin' they windows. Don't ask no questions or nothin', just start gettin' busy, man. That's how you got ta do it. Start wipin they window, they got to pay."

That black, staring like he's seen a ghost. The truck? Louise said, "Ernie, I don't like you drving Becca's truck down there. Leave it be, in the garage." Leave it be? I can't leave it be, not when she knows good as I that the killer is running loose.

That bumper sticker: "Somebody I loved was murdered." Damn, him too? Damn.

Drive by him slowly. Drive by him one more time. See if it's him. That's all, see if he's the one . . .

Hope he come back around. Give him the business, ask bout that sticker. Got my squeegee and bucket ready. This gone be a good day. Get paid, so I can go back home.

Got him. Shot the black bastard good. Got him. Now, get out of here. Louise, I got him. Becca, baby, I got him . . .

Naw! I can't believe this mess. Naw! That white . . .

But I can't tell Becca. She'd go crazy over something like this . . . She'd just given a black girl from work a lift home when it happened. Now, get away . . . now, go back to my side of town, back to Louise . . .

Iris, baby, I can't stand up. Damn. That white m'fucka set me up, like that white dude momma told me about, on the subway in New York City back in the day. White dudes just lookin to kill them a nigga.

I can't even tell Louise. She'd want to report me or something. What should I do? Go back, check on him? See if he's dead? . . . See if he's the one? Becca, I did it for you, baby. You don't know how your mom's suffered. Well, maybe you do, baby . . . Okay, okay . . .

Here he comes backin' up, fast. Guess he want to finish the job. Hope he know he might have woke somebody up, racist peckerwood bastard. Hope he know somebody might look outa window.

He's not moving. Dead? No, he's lifted his head. He's staring at me, saying something. Who the hell cares? I got him. Go, Ernest, go! Go! Leave him be. Serves him right . . . Go, Go! Go!

Come on, white man. Just a little closer. I got something for your ass. Come on.

What'd he throw just now? A wash stick and a bucket? Go! Go! Somebody will help him! Go, back to Louise and home.

Owww! Damn. Help me, somebody . . . Why's he rolling down the window? To hit me again? Damn, and I can't move . . .

"Why were you staring at my car?" The black just stares. "What did you want with my car?" He points at his leg. Looks like I shot a hole through his kneecap. No way he can walk. He motions with his head at the bucket and stick. "What did you want?"

I wanna say, "M'fucka, peckerwood bastard, look at my bucket and squeegee." Soapy water and blood all around me on this sidewalk. I wanna say, what the hell you think I want, white man? But I just stare at my work tools and fight back tears. I'm in so much pain, I don't want this white man to know.

"What's your name?"

"Ha . . . Ha . . . Harold," I say, hopin' he hear me. Hopin he don't shoot my ass again, pointing that gun like I'ma do something. Like I can do something to hurt his ass.

"Last name?"

"Steps," I say, wonderin' if he is the man or somethin'.

"Why'd you run at me like that . . . Steps?

"My business. Wipin' windows."

"It had to be more than just business, Steps, the way you stared at my vehicle, Steps. Why were you looking like that? Like I had something you wanted?

"Your bumper sticker. My momma was murdered. Young kid stabbed her." Now, I feel the tears comin' in fronta this white-m'fucka and I can't stop it. Can't stop it, missin' momma like it was yesterday.

"My daughter . . . Get in, Steps. I'll drop you off at a hospital." Leaning over, I open the passenger's door.

"I can't, I can't . . ." He ain't no cop, just a plain, old white man.

"Get in, or I'm driving off, Steps . . ." When he looks up at me, square, I can see, behind the filth and tears that he doesn't fit the description of Becca's killer.

"Help me, man."

"Come on, Steps." I can see this black is hurting badly as I watch him try to stand.

"Help me, man."

He can't. I hold open the door but he's got to make it to me on his own. No way I'm leaving the safety of my truck. That's what got Becca murdered. She walked the girl to the door and the black got her on the way back.

If I could walk, it be five, six steps, and then in, but I can't, so I got to crawl. Like in one a momma's favorite Bible stories, about Jesus and the man at the pool, who needed somebody to put him in the pool so he would be healed. Ain't nobody here, but me and him . . . So I crawl like a baby or a cripple, hopin' he don't pull off.

"Help me, man, help me."

"Hurry up, Steps, come on. Hurry up."

144

I'm thinkin' please don't pull off, whitey, but I can't say nothing. It hurts. Hurts. Damn, I don't wanna be a cripple. Now, I hold onto the car door and I can see his face good. I wanna spit in it. He's whisperin' something sound like "Becca," and somethin' else and he reaches down for me . . . and helps pull me into the car . . . Now, I'm close to him, my face next to his, and I'm fadin' . . . I want to swing on him, spit, cuss out this white peckerwood bastard, but I ain't got the strength . . . then I'm thinkin' about Iris and Ty . . . when he reaches over me to close the door, still sayin' "Becca," he drops the gun. It falls between our seats. We both reach down, towards it, and grab each other's hand, and we hold on tight as he speeds away.